PRAISE FOR *DEVIL'S PASS*
FROM **SEVEN (THE SERIES)**

"A fast-paced adventure that will keep readers on the edge of their seats...Highly Recommended."
—*CM Magazine*

"Brouwer weaves twin narratives to good effect."
—*Kirkus Reviews*

"[The] adventures are exciting and readers will be anxious to pick up the next book in the series."
—*NJ Youth Services*

PRAISE FOR *TIN SOLDIER*
FROM **THE SEVEN SEQUELS**

"A fast-paced story with lots of twists...Highly Recommended." —*CM Magazine*

"Rich in historical detail, the narrative is a crash course on a volatile time in American history. Webb...is a complicated and authentic hero."
—*Kirkus Reviews*

"Brouwer certainly knows how to weave an intriguing mystery." —*Resource Links*

BARRA CUDA

SIGMUND BROUWER

ORCA BOOK PUBLISHERS

Library and Archives Canada Cataloguing in Publication

Brouwer, Sigmund, 1959–, author
Barracuda / Sigmund Brouwer.
(The seven prequels)

Issued in print and electronic formats.
ISBN 978-1-4598-1152-2 (paperback).—ISBN 978-1-4598-1153-9 (pdf).—
ISBN 978-1-4598-1154-6 (epub)

I. Title.
PS8553.R68467B37 2016   jC813'.54   C2016-900481-3
C2016-900482-1

First published in the United States, 2016
Library of Congress Control Number: 2016933644

Summary: In this middle-grade novel, Jim Webb goes to the
Florida Keys with his grandfather and becomes embroiled in a
mystery involving a dead man and a missing cache of diamonds.

MIX
Paper from
responsible sources
FSC® C016245

*Orca Book Publishers is dedicated to preserving the environment and has
printed this book on Forest Stewardship Council® certified paper.*

Orca Book Publishers gratefully acknowledges the support for its publishing
programs provided by the following agencies: the Government of Canada
through the Canada Book Fund and the Canada Council for the Arts,
and the Province of British Columbia through the BC Arts Council
and the Book Publishing Tax Credit.

Design by Teresa Bubela
Cover photography by iStock.com
Author photo by Reba Baskett

ORCA BOOK PUBLISHERS
www.orcabook.com

Printed and bound in Canada.

19 18 17 16 • 4 3 2 1

For Brad Romans: here's to looking back at those high school days — when great rock and roll like "Barracuda" was new on eight-track tapes, and when one crazy job always seemed to lead to another even crazier than the one before.

AUTHOR'S NOTE

If you are able to, before you start reading the story, listen to the song "Barracuda" by Heart. It's the song, of course, that inspired the title of this story. Crank the music until it's obnoxiously loud. Listen to it twice and enjoy the opening guitar riffs. It will give you a sense of what it was like for Webb when he first heard that song from the bandstand.

To hear the recut version of the song, check out www.sigmundbrouwer.com/barracuda for the video that goes with this book—it sure was fun to be involved with the music.

If the real thing don't do the trick
You better make up something quick
You gonna burn, burn, burn, burn, burn to the wick
Oooh, barracuda, oh yeah *

ONE

Bad enough, Jim Webb thought, that the bright white Florida sands of his imagination didn't exist on Little Torch Key. Instead of beach, the water's edge was lined with stubby mangrove trees, thick and shrubby, that made wading through the warm water impossible. Meant he had to walk pavement, dusted with sand. To make the start of his vacation worse, though, was what waited when he finished this walk—a deathbed visit with an old man he'd never met before.

Webb was only hours off an airplane from Toronto. It was his first day of a spring vacation in the Florida Keys. The day before, he'd faced the sloppy, stained snow of crowded downtown sidewalks. Now he felt the freedom of a gentle breeze, a deep blue sky, the heat of the sun and the slap of his running shoes on pavement. He would have preferred the rhythmic lapping of waves and sand against bare toes. One thing would have been the same whether on the beach or on the road he walked. Seagulls. They squawked in circles above him, drawn by the bag of chips in his left hand.

This wasn't even close to the vacation Webb had expected. A month earlier his grandfather, David Maclean—who didn't ask it of all his grandsons but for some reason had asked Webb to call him David—had promised to take Webb on a road trip, just the two of them, as a thirteenth-birthday present.

After a month of anticipation, the trip began with a 5:00 AM goodbye to his mother on the doorstep and a taxi ride to the airport. Then the long wait at Toronto Pearson International to get through US Customs and Border Protection. Finally the time came to take off in a Boeing 767, with his grandfather beside him, telling a few war stories about when he'd flown planes small enough to land on the jet's wingspan. Their flight had landed before noon in Miami, where David had rented a Mustang convertible.

Yes. Mustang. Yes. Convertible. Yes. Cool.

Webb had ridden shotgun for a couple hours as they traveled, top down, along US Route 1 through the Florida Keys. David had explained it was called the Overseas Highway.

David had given Webb a pair of sunglasses for his birthday. They were black-lensed Oakleys, top of the line. Wearing Oakleys and riding shotgun in a convertible was much better than bumping along on an ancient streetcar in Toronto, squished between commuters with body odor.

Bridge after narrow bridge connected the small Key islands. Webb had counted down the mile markers, knowing their destination was Little Torch Key, at mile marker 28. The trip had taken them nearly a hundred miles south and west of the tip of the Florida mainland.

Still cool.

They had arrived midafternoon. They had checked in to a two-bedroom cottage at Gulfview Marina and Cottages. The view from Webb's bedroom window was grass and palm trees and shallow blue-green water beyond. David had said an old friend, Jonathan Greene, owned the resort. They were staying for free, and they'd have access to the rental fishing boats at any time. They'd even have a guide to help them land the monsters like marlin and swordfish and sailfish out in the depths of the Gulf Stream.

Better than cool. Or, as his grandfather had said, *rocking cool.* Really, rocking cool. Who else in the world ever used that phrase?

Then, as they'd unpacked their suitcases beneath the ticking of the ceiling fan in the cottage living room, David had told Webb that Jonathan Greene was in the last stages of cancer. His old friend wanted them to visit before the end of the afternoon, and David said he was glad he'd have a chance to spend time with Jonathan in the final days before the man died. And that he was glad Webb was with him during this difficult time.

Not so cool. Definitely not rocking cool.

Webb had retreated into quiet anger. He should have been told ahead of time. He should have been given a choice. Had he known David was going to force him to spend time with someone about to die, he would not have agreed to leave Toronto.

Webb usually preferred to be alone. Like now, walking on a narrow road lined with small waterfront vacation homes. When he reached the stop sign ahead at the highway, Webb would have to turn around to go make conversation with a stranger talking around oxygen tubes. Maybe there wouldn't be tubes in the guy's nose, but that's how Webb pictured the scene. Oxygen tank and horrible, wet coughs.

That was what Webb remembered of his nightmarish hospital visits to his own dad when he was six. He was too young then to really understand that his dad's cancer was an unbeatable enemy. He figured that out, though, a few months later, when he found himself in a cemetery, saying goodbye to a coffin, on an ironically beautiful fall afternoon among drifting leaves.

Trying to make idle conversation with a stranger was a torture for Webb at any time. Not much of a way to mark his birthday.

Thinking about visiting an old man on his deathbed sucked all the joy out of time in the sun. Head down, he walked in his tunnel of anger. He was on a stupid paved road. When instead he'd dreamed of sand and sun-broiled tourists, from big-bellied, balding men holding cans of beer to kids with collapsing sand castles to clusters of older teenage girls in bikinis.

That's when he heard the opening riffs of guitar that shifted his focus like he was a shark scenting blood. No, not a shark. Something else.

A barracuda.

TWO

"Barracuda."

Webb recognized the song instantly. He'd learned the chords about a year earlier, a fast-tempo crescendo that rose to a wicked slide of the electric guitar.

He saw ahead a restaurant called Mickey's Sandbar. As he reached it, he saw that the sound came from a small bandstand alongside an empty patio outside the restaurant. The bandstand was shaded by an awning. Webb could see a lone figure on the bandstand, holding a microphone.

It was too early for a real gig, Webb thought. Soundcheck maybe?

Either way, he loved hearing the song. He knew the intro riff was long. He waited for the opening words. When the words came, Webb silently sang along. He grinned at the chorus as the female singer up on the bandstand belted out the lyrics.

"You gonna burn, burn, burn, burn, burn it to the wick. Oooh, barracuda…"

At a distance, the singer was a dark outline to Webb. The music drew him closer. A couple of months earlier, he'd given up guitar. But he could still appreciate what he was hearing. She had a great voice, and those guitar riffs were classic.

It didn't take him long to reach the bandstand. He stood in the sun, still seeing the singer as a silhouette beneath the awning. The stage was set up with speakers, microphones and the snaking wires that connected it all. But she was alone. No guitar in sight. So Webb assumed it was practice for a gig later. And she was singing to a soundtrack.

"If the real thing don't do the trick, you better make up something quick…"

Without warning, she stopped.

"Hey," she said from the microphone. "What's your name?"

That's when Webb realized he was an audience of one. And he felt foolish. But she'd asked a direct question, so he felt he had no choice but to answer.

"Webb," he said. "Jim Webb."

At the hospital, about a week before the end, Webb's dad had given Webb his guitar. It was a significant gift. When Webb was five, his father had taught him his first chords. This love of music was why Webb's father had given Jim his first name in honor of a famous songwriter named Jimmy Webb. Webb preferred being called Webb, not Jim. He preferred even more not having to introduce himself to people at all.

"Well, Webb," she said, "those sunglasses are snappy, but I had to stop because you looked kinda stupid holding a bag of chips while you played air guitar."

9

He realized he must have been following the rhythm of her chords by playing it out on an imaginary guitar. That's what music did to him. Became his private universe. At least, that's what it had done for him before he'd stopped playing guitar.

Before he could say anything, she continued. "What's with the shirt?"

"Huh?" Webb looked down. He was wearing a CFL shirt.

"Eskimos."

"Oh," he said. "Edmonton Eskimos. Football team in Canada."

"Nice," she said. "Canada. Cool country."

"You sounded good," he said. She was still just an outline to him, bright sky at her back.

"You're wrong," she said. "I sounded great. It's why the bar pays me to sing at night even though I'm only fifteen. And I'm going to kick butt in the Battle of the Bands next week. You make sure that you're here to vote for me."

"If I can," Webb said. It was supposed to be a ten-day trip.

"You actually play guitar?" she asked. "Or is that air guitar a wannabe thing?"

He was about to say no, he didn't play guitar. Which would have been the truth. He didn't play anymore.

Before he could tell her anything, she stepped away from the microphone into the light. She stopped being an outline. Webb almost dropped his bag of chips.

Webb had never paid much attention to girls. At least, not in the sense of the boy-girl thing. But that changed now in an instant. He saw blond hippie-style hair that framed a gorgeous face and deep-brown eyes. He saw the tight jeans and the tube top that exposed her tanned midriff. He understood that in his entire life he'd been unaware of an entirely new universe called L-O-V-E. In that moment, his thirteenth birthday became a day he knew he'd remember for the rest of his life. No, it became a day he'd cherish for the rest of his life. Not even spending part of his thirteenth birthday with a stranger on his deathbed

11

would ruin this day. He knew this was a girl he'd rescue from dragons in each and every daydream about her.

"I play guitar," Webb answered. He would admit he ate live worms to get her approval, if that's what she wanted.

"Then come up and show me," she said, grinning. "I'm tired of practicing to a sound-track, and chances are, I can sing to whatever you play."

Perfect. He could switch from a knight in shining armor to a dude blowing her away with guitar licks.

"I can play 'Barracuda,'" Webb said.

"You rock," she answered. Webb tried not to wriggle like a puppy getting his head scratched.

Webb floated up the steps of the bandstand. Floated. Really. He was goofy, insane, big-time crushing. First. Time. Ever. This was so amazing, he was almost ready to become talkative.

"I'm Kristie," she said. "Nice to meet you."

Kristie had said she was fifteen. She had real stage presence though. He wanted to rush to a flower store and come back with a dozen roses to lay at her feet.

She reached to a guitar stand and lifted a gleaming, jet-black electric. A Strat. Nice guitar.

She stretched it toward him with a perfectly formed hand. It was attached to a perfectly formed arm, and the arm was attached to a perfectly formed shoulder. It was as perfectly formed as her other hand and arm and shoulder. It was just as perfectly formed as everything else about her. Yeah, Webb thought, now I get the whole Romeo-and-Juliet thing. Give me some moonlight, and I'll start singing to her.

He hoped nothing about his exterior betrayed these thoughts and was glad for his dark sunglasses.

Be cool, he told himself. Be cool.

He strapped on the guitar. He flicked through the strings, checking by ear to make sure they were tuned.

Okay, he told himself, blow her away. "Barracuda."

A smile of anticipation played across Kristie's face.

Webb hit the first chord, and the music died. It took him a second to realize that the power had been cut to the speakers.

As he looked over his shoulder, he saw someone at the back of the stage. A guy, late teens. The guy had ripped arms and chest, displayed by a T-shirt with cut-off sleeves. He was holding the end of the extension cord and had obviously just yanked it from the outlet. He also had a snarl on his face.

"Sylas," Kristie said.

"Don't *Sylas* me," he said. "Tell me what's going on. The guy's got my guitar."

"Just checking this guy out in case we need a backup."

"We don't," Sylas said. "Get rid of him."

Sylas spoke as if Webb wasn't there.

Webb wasn't going to react in any way, because he refused to give Sylas that kind of satisfaction. And he sure wasn't going to make Kristie tell him to go.

He set down the guitar and walked.

THREE

When Webb reached the cottage, the palm-tree shadows stretched across the grass. The shapes of the fronds almost reached the patio where his grandfather sat in one of two identical lawn chairs. The chairs were the type with wide arms and built-in cup holders. A tall glass of iced lemonade filled the holder on the right arm of David's chair. The glass was beaded with moisture. A small black transistor radio rested in the other cup holder. The speaker was tilted upward, with jazz music crackling at low volume.

David had a novel in his hands. It was by Jack London. *The Call of the Wild*. David had been reading it on the airplane. David said he loved Canada's north and that Webb should make it a point to go there someday.

Now he gave Webb a nod.

"Did that walk get it out of your system?" David asked. His voice was calm. It was always calm.

Webb stood in one spot and sifted through his possible answers. Because his stepdad made life miserable for him, Webb was an expert at this game.

Saying yes would be an admission there had been something bothering him but that it was such a small deal a walk could get rid of it.

Saying no would show how unfair this deathbed surprise had been. But then David would want to discuss it. Webb was in no mood to share his feelings. Ever.

If Webb answered by asking, *Get what out of my system?*, it would also lead to discussion.

The best way to play it was to change the subject and not answer the question.

Webb said, "Am I dressed okay for meeting your old friend?"

David was wearing khaki pants and a loose Hawaiian shirt with muted colors and a patterns of flying parrots. David was a tall man with lots of hair, and he was trim and fit. People knew he was old. The flowing hair was nearly white, and there was no hiding his wrinkles. But he moved with the gracefulness of a younger man and spoke with an energetic vibration in his voice.

"We're in the Keys," David said, as if he hadn't noticed that Webb had not answered the first question. "I think your T-shirt and shorts and sandals are the dress code for nearly anything. My generation does think it's rude to hide your eyes during conversation, but that's your call. I'm good either way."

Webb knew how he was going to play this now. Like he was happy and nothing bothered him. But that wouldn't change how mad he was.

Seriously, springing a deathbed scene on him after Webb had landed in Florida?

"Thanks for the reminder," Webb said. He took off the sunglasses and flipped them around, as if he had eyes in the back of his head. "Great present by the way. Thanks."

Yeah. Webb would play it happy in the presence of his grandfather. But Webb would do his best to find as much alone time as possible.

"I am impressed by your sudden fake cheerfulness," David said. "I can see why you drive your stepfather crazy."

Webb realized he should never forget how quick his grandfather was.

"I didn't know this trip was about getting me alone so you could grill me about my life," Webb said. "I thought it was some kind of tradition that you had for your grandsons. A fun trip."

"That's the tradition," David said. He sipped from his lemonade and smiled. "Although I was the one who suggested the Florida Keys. Didn't you once mention Italy?"

"I'm good with Florida," Webb said. It looked as if he was clear of the stepfather conversation at this point. Now that Webb could see what the game was, he was going to be like Teflon. Let everything slide off him like it didn't matter. Besides, he'd find ways to get back to the bandstand and see Kristie again. Nothing like L-O-V-E to make time fly.

Webb continued, "We've got a great place to stay, and it will be fun to go fishing in the gulf, right?"

He paused, like something had just occurred to him, and then said, "Hey, wasn't your friend expecting us about now?"

That should definitely take them away from any conversations about Webb's stepfather.

"I don't think he'll croak before we get there," David said. "How about you sit for a minute or two and let me tell you about him?"

"Sure," Webb said. "Maybe I can grab a lemonade first?"

"It's in the fridge. Should have had it ready for you," his grandfather said. He waved lazily toward the cottage door. "I'll be waiting right here."

Webb wandered into the kitchen of the small cottage and pretended to look for a glass, even though he knew where they were. The trick was to take enough time to make the adult mad, but not so much time that the adult could accuse you of dragging it out without looking like an idiot. It was the only way Webb survived life at home, enjoying how it felt to irritate his stepfather without pushing him over the tipping point of anger.

But here, Webb was conflicted. His grandfather was a great guy. Webb loved him as much as he could love an old man he saw about once a month. More important, Webb respected David, not something he could say about his stepfather.

Part of him wanted to go back out to the patio to hug his grandfather and apologize for the attitude. The other part wanted to lock himself in his bedroom. The school counselor had talked lots about a flood of hormones that came with adolescence and how that led teenagers to be overwhelmed by confusing feelings. Webb hated listening to his school counselor. Maybe that came with hormones too.

The crackly jazz music drifted into the small kitchen. The image of his grandfather sitting in the chair, calmly smiling, felt so good to Webb that he blinked away the beginning of tears. Stupid hormones. Stupid school counselor.

Webb decided to pick up the pace so David didn't have to wait.

He walked back into the warm humidity and slipped into the other chair. It was just far enough away from David that Webb didn't feel uncomfortable.

"So," Webb said, "tell me about your friend Jonathan Greene."

"Sure," David said. "Either he is losing his mind, or someone is trying to steal everything he took a lifetime to build."

FOUR

"I've told you enough stories about my own life," David said from his lawn chair, "so apologies that I have yet another for you."

Webb spoke the truth. "I never get tired of your stories."

Webb knew his grandfather was a remarkable man by any measure. He had been a lifelong adventurer, all the way back to fighting in the Spanish Civil War. From there, David had been shot down while flying airplanes in World War II. He had been to dozens of countries since. Every once in a while, people joked that David McLean must have been a spy, for all the places he had been and the famous people he knew.

"Here are my World War Two flying buddies," David said. He lifted *The Call of the Wild* from his lap and opened it. He pulled out a black-and-white photo and handed it to Webb.

The photo showed four young men in airforce uniforms, grinning. Webb only recognized one of the men, his grandfather. They were standing in front of a biplane on a grass runway. The wings and the upper body of the airplane were black. The lower half was pale. It was a black-and-white photo, so Webb couldn't be sure of the plane's real color.

"That's a de Havilland Tiger Moth from the 1930s," David said. "Canadian-manufactured plane. It was used as a military trainer aircraft for a lot of countries. The four of us cut our teeth on that plane. Me. Jake Rundell. Harlowe Gavin. Ray Daley."

"Not Jonathan Greene?"

"Rundell and Daley are still alive," David said. "We find ways to get together now and then.

Air shows, things like that. Harlowe Gavin, that's a story for another day. I don't expect you to remember their names or their faces though. What's important about the photo is that the person behind the camera was Jonathan Greene."

"So you were a group of five friends?"

"Not exactly," David said. "Jonathan Greene trained with us. But he never really fit in. He never stepped into photographs. Never went out with us on our free time. We thought he was arrogant and a jerk. Took me a long time to realize how wrong we were."

David slid the photograph back into his novel and set the book on his lap. "Wasn't until then that I made sure to look him up and apologize. That might have been thirty years after the war. Fact is, we all owed him a lot for how he quietly helped all the time even when we made him feel like an outsider."

"Outsider?"

"We should have made him one of us. We didn't understand that some people…"

25

David paused, then appeared to switch directions. "Did you know that there are three kinds of people in the world?"

Webb waited for the answer.

David said, "Those who can do math and those who can't."

Webb squinted.

"I know," David said. "Bad joke."

"No," Webb said a second later, after thinking it through. "Actually a pretty good joke. Just came out of nowhere, that's all."

"Where it came from was that I want to explain how you really can divide people into one of two types. Introvert or extrovert. A psychiatrist name Carl Jung said there is no such thing as a pure introvert or extrovert. Such a person would be in the lunatic asylum. So while everyone has a little of both, a person will fall on one side or the other of being an extrovert or an introvert. If you understand that, then things you do and things others do will make more sense to you. A lot of people say extroverts are loud and sociable and that introverts are quiet and shy. But it's not that simple."

"Something tells me you're going to explain."

"Extroverts gain energy from other people. That's where they get their kicks. From people and from activity. Like parties. I'm an extrovert. That's why I'm always busy. I love meeting new people, trying new things. As for introverts…let me ask you this. Wonder why I ask you to call me David instead of Grandfather or Granddad?"

"Nope."

"Want to explain why you don't wonder?"

"Nope."

"See? You're a guarded type of person. Walled. You like keeping people out. I don't ask my other grandsons to call me David, but I think you like the distance and feel better that way. And I'm good with that."

"Boy," Webb said. "Getting late. How about we get the visit over with?"

"And that speaks volumes. That you think about a visit to someone you don't know as

27

something you need to get over with. Like it's a chore. Is it safe to say you don't like meeting new people?"

"I'd rather push a needle into my eyeball," Webb said sourly. "I have an idea. How about I visit someone I've never met before and talk to him while he's dying?"

His grandfather laughed. And speaking his resentment out loud had made Webb feel better, like he'd just pulled out a sliver.

"Introverts need time alone," David said. "They aren't necessarily shy, because shyness implies a fear of social encounters. Introverts need solitude to recharge their batteries, and being around people constantly drains them. It's the reverse for extroverts. I get charged back up by being around people."

"I don't mind being around you," Webb said. "Just in case you were going to call me an introvert."

"I'm glad. Introverts are great with one-on-one conversations with people they trust.

But you said that like being an introvert is a bad thing. And that's one of my points. We're in a society that celebrates extroverts, which tends to make introverts feel out of place. How do you like school?"

"Huh?" Webb said. This was a fast-moving conversation.

"I'll answer for you," David said. "I talked to your mother. She says you hate school. And now let me tell you why. It's because of the group work you face every day."

"Huh?"

"Pods," David said. "Your teacher, believing it's important to teach kids how to work in teams, has put four desks together to create pods, and so the kids work in groups. Great for extroverts. Not so great for introverts if the teacher isn't aware of what introverts need. Some teachers think you have to force kids out of their shells. But what if the kid is wired to work better when he's alone and can focus on stuff instead of trying to shut out all the distractions?"

"Huh," Webb said. Things were making sense to him now. He was in a classroom with pods. He did hate school because of it. He did like to work on things alone. He did need solitude to get his energy back. His teacher was always trying to prod him to be more of a team player, as if Webb was a jerk for keeping to himself.

"Huh," Webb said again. Then he gave his grandfather a suspicious look. "You planned a conversation like this with me, didn't you?"

"I'm your grandfather," David said. "It's part of the job description."

"But we're good for the rest of the trip, right? No more talks like this?"

"Not unless you bring it up." David grinned. "Or I change my mind."

"Great," Webb said sarcastically. "So, Jonathan Greene?"

"Introvert. Hardworking, honest. Brilliant. Problem solver. Even a great leader. A couple of times, we wouldn't have survived our missions without him stepping up to the plate and taking over."

"Introverts can be leaders?" Webb asked.

"Often better than extroverts. Introverts listen. I really hope you can understand that being an introvert is a positive thing."

"I thought we weren't going to be discussing me anymore."

"I thought I reserved the right to change my mind," David said. "See how lovable we extroverts are?"

"If your friend is an introvert, why would he own a resort?" Webb said, choosing to ignore his grandfather's charming grin. "That means dealing with people all the time."

"It's always been on his terms," David answered. "At least, until his illness took away his independence. That's why I asked you to come to the Keys with me. My apology never felt like enough. He needs our help, and I owe him."

David opened his novel again. This time he pulled out a folded piece of paper from the pages instead of a photograph.

"Greene sent me this book, you know," David said. "At the beginning of the second chapter, I found a note glued to the page. This one."

The handwriting was faint and the letters were ragged, as if written by a shaky hand.

Webb read the note. Three sentences.

They are trying to steal everything. Help. I'm not safe in my own home.

FIVE

The scene at the bedside was everything Webb had expected and feared. Oxygen tank, tubes in nose, wheezing.

What he had not expected was the panic in Jonathan Greene's eyes when the old man momentarily stopped breathing.

They are trying to steal everything. Help. I'm not safe in my own home.

Webb had walked with David to a mansion among palm trees on the water's edge, just down from the resort. A middle-aged woman had met them at the door and told them she was Yvonne Delta, Greene's full-time nurse.

She had taken them inside, saying very little. The big house had windows that took in the view, and hardwood floors in every room. There was no trace of dust anywhere. The art on the walls showed the brush lines of oil paintings, not the flatness of cheap reproductions. There were small statues of animals on burnished wood shelves.

Without speaking, Yvonne had opened the door to Jonathan Greene's bedroom and pointed inside, where Webb had his first look at the dying man.

The old man was dressed in light-green pajamas. His head seemed huge compared to his shrunken body. Webb had seen photographs of a younger Greene. This man was a shell. Sunken cheeks, only wisps of hair that had once been wavy.

He lay in his bed in a large bedroom that had another huge window with another great view of the bay. On their arrival, Greene had slowly reached over for a remote control and raised the top half of the mattress, to put him in a near-sitting position.

He'd then set the remote beside a digital picture frame on the bedside table that showed a new photo every ten seconds or so.

They are trying to steal everything. Help. I'm not safe in my own home.

David had waved Webb to stay put, then moved forward, leaned close to Greene and had a whispered conversation that finished with a gentle hug. David had then pulled two chairs up to the bed and taken one. Webb had been invited forward to sit on a chair beside David, and after Webb had seated himself, Greene had begun to gasp for air.

That's when Webb saw panic in Greene's eyes.

"He needs help!" Webb said, feeling panic himself. The old man was going to die right in front of him.

Greene waved it away.

"No," David said. "It will pass."

Greene managed to nod, but it didn't take away the fear in his eyes, the fear of a drowning man. A few agonizing seconds later, Greene found air again.

"Nothing to worry about," Greene managed in a hoarse whisper. "That's the way it is."

"No need to apologize," David said. He grabbed a tissue from a box at the bedside and used it to wipe away some spit at Greene's mouth. "It's not something you choose."

Greene choked on a snort. "If I could choose, there would be about a thousand better ways to do this."

His eyes turned to Webb. "So you're the grandson he's been talking about. I can honestly say I've been dying to meet you."

Webb couldn't help it. He laughed. That was something else he hadn't expected at a deathbed. Jokes. So if these two old men weren't going to flinch or feel sorry for themselves, neither would Webb.

"Nice to meet you too," Webb said. "Thanks for a great place to stay."

"Never got tired of it," Greene said. "You'll be out on the gulf tomorrow. Lock it into your memory."

"Yes, sir," Webb said. But Webb couldn't help but think of the note.

They are trying to steal everything. Help. I'm not safe in my own home.

"I can tell you he's already locked something else into his memory," David said. "A girl belting out some rock and roll at a beachside bar."

"Hey," Webb said.

David spoke to Greene. "I managed to get him to tell me about her. Just watching the grin on his face when he talked about…" David snapped his fingers. "Webb, what's the girl's name?"

"Got to be Kristie," Greene told David. "Kristie McCullough. Local girl. Wants to be a singer. This is a small key. We know everybody."

"Kristie," David said. "That's her. Right, Webb?"

"See if I tell you anything again," Webb said.

Greene coughed and said, "Kristie's something, all right. If I were fifty years younger…"

David said, "Nice try. You'd have to be sixty-five years younger for her to look at you twice.

Maybe seventy. Then you'd be back around Webb's age."

"Ain't that the truth," Greene said. He looked at Webb. "I probably don't have to tell you, but run hard while you can. When you get to where I am, you'll want to know that you squeezed everything you could out of life."

Greene's smiled faded. When it did, it seemed like the old man's face collapsed in on itself.

He coughed for another few seconds that to Webb seemed like hours. Greene was desperate for air. When he finished, he found enough energy to say, "Was hoping I might be in better shape for this conversation."

"Take your time," David said.

"That's my point." Greene's voice was weak. "Not much left. And I need to fix something before I go. I've made a mess of my life."

"Doesn't look like it," David said.

"That's the thing about appearances. We all have our secrets."

Secrets, Webb thought. And thought again of the note. *They are trying to steal everything. Help. I'm not safe in my own home.*

"Tell me how we can help," David said.

Greene tried to answer, but another spasm of coughing hit him.

Again, when it was over, David reached for a tissue, but this time he gave it to Webb.

Webb froze and didn't take the tissue. He didn't want to touch a dying man.

David gave him an unblinking look, then wiped the spittle from Greene's mouth.

"Thanks," Greene said.

"Tell me how we can help," David repeated.

"Make sure everything I have goes to the charity that I put in my will. It's called Operation Smile. Helps kids with surgery. I don't have family, and maybe it will make up for the horrible thing I did when…"

Greene coughed again. David wiped his face again.

"Lawyers are there to make sure that your will is executed properly," David said. "And if you want to talk, I'm here to listen."

"I only trust you to get the diamonds," Greene told David. "Those need to go to Operation Smile. Anyone else would steal them. Once you find the first tin, I'll tell you where you can find the rest."

"Diamonds?" David asked.

Greene sucked in air and tried to find energy. He patted his chest.

"I've hidden a letter here. Grab it, David."

Webb's grandfather unbuttoned the pajama top, pulled a paper out and rebuttoned the top.

"When you get back to the cottage, read it," Greene said. "Let's talk tomorrow." He managed a sad smile. "If I don't make it through the night, do your best to sort things out."

"That's what we're here for, my friend." David patted the man's hand. "I'm honored at the chance to help."

Greene began to cough again and waved them away. Webb's last view was that expression again, the fear of a man about to sink beneath the waves.

SIX

The thunderstorm began just after Webb and David made it back to their cottage, with lightning flicking over the water and the rain coming in sideways.

"Heat," Webb's grandfather said, glancing out the window. "Sometimes it just needs a release like this."

The frequent flashes of white came like a strobe light, and the peals of thunder like ominous drums.

"Before I read Greene's letter," David said, "you should know something about the final days for a lot of people. Especially older people. They often become delusional because their brains stop functioning properly. They may babble. They deserve compassion and empathy, because it's real to them. But that doesn't mean we need to take what they say seriously."

"But I thought you came down because he needed help," Webb said.

"Yes, but not the help he thinks he needs," David answered. "He has no family. A man shouldn't have to die alone."

Thoughts of his own dad in the hospital hit Webb, and with them the anger that always came too. If his dad hadn't died, Webb wouldn't be stuck in a miserable life with a stepfather like—

"No time like the present," David said, interrupting Webb's thoughts.

David was sitting on the end of the couch near a lamp. He flicked it on, unfolded some reading glasses, then opened the letter.

"Hmmm," David said. It had not taken him long to read the letter.

"Hmmm?"

David opened his mouth to speak, and a crackle of lightning stopped him. The boom of the thunder was so loud and close that it rattled the windows of the cottage.

"Hmmm?" Webb said again.

"Read it for yourself."

Webb scooted closer to the lamp and took the paper from his grandfather.

Lightning flicked a few more times before he reached the end of the words.

I need the pills because everything hurts so bad. But when I take the pills, I go into dreams where I'm awake. It's like being in a fog. I hear voices, and the voices ask me questions again and again. About the diamonds.

To put the note into the book that I sent, I had to pretend to take those pills so my mind was clear. I glued the note so she wouldn't find it. But the pain is unbearable. So I take the pills, and the fog and the voices return.

This morning, I threw the pills away so I could write this letter.

Stop the voices for me.

Find the box of diamonds and bring it to me so that the voices will let me die in peace. In the bathroom of your cottage, behind the toilet, find the cinder block that's loose. The box is hidden in the hollow center of the cinder block.

"Diamonds," Webb said to his grandfather. "In this cottage."

"He's owned the resort for decades," David answered. "I suppose this would be as safe a place as any. If the diamonds exist."

"Might be a delusion?"

The rain abruptly stopped rattling the windows, and Webb felt less spooked by the situation.

His grandfather gave a grin. "One way to find out. I'll let you do the work though. My knees aren't what they used to be."

Webb forced himself to walk slowly to the bathroom. Diamonds.

His grandfather followed.

Webb was wearing shorts. The tile floor was cool to the skin of his knees. The bathroom was against the outside wall of the cottage, which was made of cinder blocks. Webb began pushing at the blocks.

One moved.

The light was dim behind the toilet. Webb could see there was no way to wiggle the block out. Then he noticed a small hole in the center of the block.

"Hmmm," Webb said.

"Hmmm?" his grandfather asked.

"If there's a mouse nest hidden back there, I hope I don't lose my finger," Webb said.

He pushed his index finger into the hole and was able to curl the finger against the back side of the cinder block. It took effort, and the edge of the hole put painful pressure against the inside of his finger, but he was able to slide the block out.

His grandfather was leaning over Webb's shoulders.

"Hmmm," his grandfather said.

"I agree," Webb said. Inside the hollow part of the block was a small tin cigar box.

Diamonds.

Except when Webb opened it, the box was completely empty.

SEVEN

In the first groggy moments of coming out of sleep, Webb thought the *tap-tap-tap* sound at his bedroom window came from rain.

Moonlight, however, showed the shape of shoulders and a head, and Webb let his thoughts clear without moving his body. He wanted to figure out what was happening before he let whoever it was realize that he was awake. He could feel his heart rate accelerate as he fought his fear.

Tap. Tap. Tap.

Webb's heart rate leapt to any entirely new level. But not because the person at the window

was a threat. She'd shifted slightly, and the moonlight had given him enough detail to recognize
her face.

Kristie. Kristie McCullough.

Webb was glad he usually slept in sweat shorts
and a T-shirt. He slid out of bed, moved to the
window and opened it.

"Hey," he whispered.

"Hey," she whispered back.

"How did you know I was here?" Webb asked.

"Small island," she said. "Easy to find out.
Want to sneak out?"

"Huh?"

"Come on out," she said. "Walk along the
water. I owe you an apology for today."

"Um…"

"Good. I'll wait by the water."

She stepped away and seemed to flow into the
shadows.

Webb wondered if he needed David's permission for this. Probably. A glance at the alarm clock
on the bedside table showed that it was 2:18 AM.

Late night, early morning. But if David said no, then what? Maybe better just to go for a walk and tell David after. That way he could be honest with his grandfather and still be able to spend time in the moonlight with Kristie.

Moonlight. Florida waters. Wow.

Webb was tempted to go out the window. But he decided he didn't like being a sneak. He'd go out the cottage door, enjoy the walk and in the morning tell his grandfather about it.

Good plan, Webb thought. Nothing can go wrong.

He threw on blue jeans but stayed in the T-shirt he'd worn to bed. He slipped into sandals and opened his bedroom door. He could hear snoring coming from behind the other bedroom door.

He told himself it would be rude to wake his grandfather. Webb was thirteen now, old enough to walk at night.

Webb was still quiet about unlatching the door to the outside patio. And quiet about shutting it.

He knew he was trying to fool himself. It was sneaky. But he would do it anyway.

With the thunderstorm long passed, the moonlight was bright enough to cast shadows, and the edges of the palm leaves etched onto the sand looked like saw blades.

Webb walked over those shadows, his sandals crunching on the tiny shells of long-dead crustaceans mixed into the sand.

For a moment he didn't see Kristie. For a moment he wondered if this was a trap. After all, what if the threats in Jonathan Greene's letters were not the fevered imaginings of a man close to death?

It was a little late for those thoughts, Webb told himself.

Kristie's voice reached him.

"Over here," she said.

He turned. There she was.

Moonlight. Water's edge. Wow.

He walked to her, and she reached out a hand. He'd never held hands with a girl before. Never.

It messed with his head. He hoped his palms wouldn't sweat.

She pulled his hand, and he followed and they began to walk. Beyond the mangroves, the view of the bay under the moonlight was spectacular.

"Sorry if I woke you," she said. "I'm a night owl."

"Me too," Webb said, wondering what power she had to make him blurt that without a second's thought. He wasn't a night person. He was usually awake and out of bed at 6:00 AM, which was weird for a teenager.

"The water always puts me in a good mood," she said.

"Me too," he said. Water was okay, but not something to swoon over. But if she liked water, he liked water.

Moonlight. Florida ocean. Holding hands. Wow.

"You should come by and play guitar sometime," Kristie said. "Sylas was just in a bad mood today."

"He's in your band?"

"He's in *the* band. He doesn't have my kind of dreams. Someday I want to be in Nashville. Where the music is. He just wants to hang out in the Keys. Fish. Stay lazy. How about you? What do you want?"

Webb shrugged. This was crazy. He was holding hands. With a G-I-R-L, but he still felt like he needed to keep his thoughts and feelings private. His grandfather was right. Webb was a guarded type of person. Maybe he did need to learn how to open up to other people.

She didn't seem mad that he hadn't answered, but she changed the subject.

"Someone at the bar said you and your grandfather are visiting Jonathan Greene," she said.

"Yes," Webb said. This didn't involve sharing anything like feelings.

"He doesn't have long," she said. "Everybody says that."

Webb thought of how David had wiped spittle off the old man's face.

"Yes," Webb said.

"When he goes," Kristie said, "I guess his secret will go with him."

"Secret?" Webb said, thinking of the empty tin in the cinder block.

They were walking slowly.

"Everyone says that when he was a kid, he found some kind of treasure. But instead of making some big claim, he kept it hidden and just took out a little at a time. That's how he built up all his money. Think that's true?"

Webb said, "I just got here with my grandfather, so I don't really know."

"Well, maybe he's going to spill it on his deathbed. You know, like some kind of confession. Wouldn't that be cool? I mean, did he tell you anything? Give you anything?"

Before Webb could answer, he heard a loud snap somewhere behind him in the darkness.

He turned, pulling his fingers away from Kristie's. He saw nothing of danger among the trees. Still, it felt like they were being watched.

Kristie just kept walking. He caught up to her. She didn't reach for his hand, and he was too shy to reach for hers.

"Well?" Kristie asked.

"Maybe an animal or something," Webb said. While the waterfront was cleared of mangroves, the rest of the resort had shrubs and bushes as part of the landscaping. Easy enough for a raccoon or something to hide.

"Not well what was the noise. I mean about Jonathan Greene. You haven't heard anything, have you?"

"I just got here with my grandfather," Webb said again. Guarded again. Like it was instinct.

She let out a deep breath. "Well, thanks," she said.

"Thanks?"

"You helped me clear my head with this walk. I'm ready to crash now. That was nice of you. So maybe see you at the Sandbar for Battle of the Bands?"

She waved goodbye.

Goodbye?

Webb didn't move.

"You don't need help getting back to your cottage, do you?" she said.

"No."

"Good. Because I'm headed home."

Just like that, it was over. The moonlight. The water's edge. And the wow.

EIGHT

When Webb's alarm went off at 6:00 AM, he felt like he'd only had a few hours' sleep. Then he realized that was because he *had* only had a few hours' sleep, and the moonlight walk with Kristie had not been a dream.

He hit the Snooze button but didn't fall back to sleep. His feelings about Kristie were mixed up, and he wanted to try to sort them out. On the one hand, she had woken him up in the middle of the night to go for a walk. On the other hand, it seemed like she had instantly lost interest in walking with him. What had he done wrong?

As he stared at the ceiling, trying to remember every moment with Kristie, his grandfather knocked on the door.

"Jack England is on the patio," David said. "He's going to feed us breakfast on the boat. Time to catch a marlin."

Marlin. That would be one of those eight-hundred-pound fish. Webb could picture it jumping from the water as it tried to throw the hook. Very. Cool.

Webb rolled onto the floor and was ready in the time it took to brush his teeth, run wet fingers through his hair and step into shorts, T-shirt and sandals.

When he stepped into the humid air of a Florida morning, David was sitting in a patio chair, sipping tea. In the other chair, where Webb had sat the night before, was a man that Webb guessed to be in his late fifties.

The man turned his head and gave Webb a smile. He was taller than Webb by a few inches. His face was deeply tanned. He was smoking a hand-rolled cigarette. He wore jeans and a faded denim shirt stained with salt. His feet were bare in rubber-soled shoes with canvas tops.

"Jack England." The man extended his hand. "England more than Jack."

Webb took it. The man's skin was rough and his fingers strong.

"Jim Webb," Webb said. "Webb more than Jim."

"Webb, huh," Jack said. He took a final drag from his cigarette, dropped it on the patio stones and gave it a quick grind with his right heel. It left a swirl of blackened tobacco about the twice the size of a quarter.

"Well, Webb," England said, "we need to move. It's a charter, and the others will probably be there waiting for us."

"Others?" Webb said.

"Greene might be on his way out," England said, "but he still runs a tight business. We're happy to give the two of you a day on the boat, but we can't run it without the paying customers.

Don't worry. It's a big boat with lots of room. It has to be big. We won't go into the Gulf Stream in anything under forty feet."

England stood up.

"The Gulf Stream is like a river in the Atlantic," he explained as the three of them walked down a path between the resort's cottages to the marina. "It's a few miles offshore, and when we hit it, the current is strong. Stretches about forty to sixty miles wide and over a half mile deep. Flows north at a good five miles an hour. You don't want to be in the stream in a small boat, but if you want big fish, that's where you need to go."

The sun was hot already as England talked. He seemed like a man who liked to fill silences.

"I'm a believer that out on the water, problems come in threes," England said. "One little thing happens and that sets off a chain reaction of problems. Say your bilge pump stops working because of a wire corroded by seawater, then—"

"Bilge pump?" Webb asked.

"Pumps out seawater that gets into the boat. Bilge pump maybe goes, and then an engine or two floods. You don't want that when you're in the Gulf Stream. I've seen it plenty. One loose wire and a couple hours later you're hoping for a helicopter rescue at sea. If you're lucky enough to still be floating."

England laughed and said, "I hope I'm not scaring you."

David smiled. "Webb doesn't scare easily. And me, I figure if you're part of Jonathan Greene's team, I can trust you as much as I'd trust him."

England nodded. "You're going to have a good day. I'll be skippering the boat, so I can promise everything will be great."

Webb was prepared to accept that, except when they reached the marina, some men were gathered on a dock by the largest boat, a boom box at their feet, thumping out obnoxious country tunes.

Country music itself wasn't obnoxious to Webb. But the stuff that celebrated redneck drinking didn't do a lot for him. These guys—a half dozen, one of them wearing a shirt that showed the Confederate flag—were cracking open beers to match the music.

Webb felt his gut tighten. Sure, the boat was big enough. But that wouldn't be big enough for him. He could imagine what it would be like out in the Atlantic, no land in sight, trapped by party music and drunk party jokes.

"England?" Webb said.

The man stopped. They were still twenty paces from the boat and the party guys who were ready to combine beer and big-game fishing.

"Jonathan Greene told us yesterday that we could use any of the resort equipment," Webb said.

"Told me too," England said. "That's why we're sending you in the best boat we have."

"I'm thinking," Webb said, "I'd prefer something else."

Webb pointed down the dock, where boats of various sizes bobbed in the water. To one that was bright yellow, the tiniest craft of all of them.

A one-person kayak.

NINE

"Kayak," England said. There was disbelief in his voice. "You're pointing at a kayak."

"I watched some videos on YouTube," Webb said. "About fishing the shallow waters of the Keys. Doesn't look like it could get me into trouble. The water isn't deep enough to hold sharks. All I need is a fishing rod with a lure, and the kayak."

Webb gave England the most charming grin he could. "And maybe the breakfast and lunch you packed."

England frowned. "That wasn't the plan. I was supposed to take you and your grandfather out into the Gulf Stream." He pointed at the huge boat. "How could a kid like you not want to go out in something like that? The horsepower is incredible. See all those fishing poles? We bait them for you with bigger fish than you'd catch in the shallows. All you do is wait for a strike and then you get to fight a game fish. How cool is that?"

Not very, Webb wanted to say. Have a guide do all the work? Sit around and listen to bad jokes told by other guys who wanted the guide to do all the work? Putting up with a big noisy engine instead of calm, quiet waters?

"Sounds okay," Webb said. "But I'd prefer the kayak. And I read in the brochure that all the resort watercraft have GPS locators to make sure nobody gets lost."

"Won't be possible," England said. "I'm sure your grandfather wanted to share a special day on the water with you."

David broke in. "Grandfather is right here. Grandfather doesn't need a charter. Grandfather is happy to go back to the cottage and read a book for most of the day. Grandfather thinks that if Grandson wants an adventure in a kayak, then Grandson should get that adventure. And Grandfather thinks that if this resort won't arrange it, Grandfather will go down the road to another resort and rent a kayak."

David paused and smiled at England. But it was a cold smile, showing that David didn't tolerate people messing with him. "Was Grandfather clear?"

England grunted. "You don't know what you're missing. The Gulf Stream is amazing."

"So Grandfather wasn't clear?" David asked.

One of the group of beer drinkers shouted at England. "Hey, aren't we running behind? For the price we paid, this boat should be headed out already."

Before England could reply, a voice from behind them answered.

"We'll head out now!"

Webb glanced over and saw another man, younger than England but with the same deep tan and wrinkles that would match in a few years. This man, too, had on a hat with the resort logo. He had a huge mermaid tattoo on his right forearm, with bright blues and greens and purples that glowed like neon.

The man offered England a high five. "Sorry for the delay. But I'm good to take them. You help the kid with his kayak."

"No!" England said sharply. "Robbie, that charter was on the books for me today."

"So you'll be the one to let Jonathan Greene know you walked away from his special guests? There's a man you don't want angry at you, even when he's dying."

"I can get the kid ready in his kayak in about two minutes," England said. "Then I'll take the charter out."

"Hey," another one of the beer drinkers yelled. "We're wasting daylight!"

"Two minutes too long," Robbie said. "Don't worry, England, I have you covered."

"But—"

"Just help the kid with his kayak. Make sure you put a wire-tipped leader on his line."

With that, Robbie bounced forward and herded all the beer drinkers on board. England stared, arms crossed, with obvious frustration as Robbie jumped onto the boat and ran through the checklist. Within minutes he had thrown the ropes clear and backed the large boat into the center of the marina, and then, with a cheery wave, he throttled the boat forward and out to the open waters.

"Sorry about that," Webb said. "I didn't want to cause any trouble."

England grunted.

Webb said, "It would be great if you just gave me some basic instructions and let me go out myself."

Last thing Webb wanted was to be stuck with England for a morning.

"I can't just give you a kayak and let you paddle around," England said.

"Yes," David said. "You can. With the GPS locator, he'll be fine."

Webb's grandfather suddenly seemed twenty years younger. And taller. Webb realized that he'd never seen his grandfather like this. Quietly angry.

"Not only *can* you let him jump in a kayak," David continued, "you *will.*"

England seemed like he was about to disagree, but he must have seen the steel in David's posture.

"Fine then," England said. "I take no responsibility. The kid doesn't make it back, it's on your shoulders."

TEN

Half an hour later, Webb paddled to the shoreline nearest to their cottage, where his grandfather stood waiting.

Webb was wearing a life jacket, and he felt comfortable. He loved the kayak.

The seat cushion was set in front of a storage box, and he'd learned he could easily turn and reach it. There was spare rod in a rod holder attached to the storage box, and the storage box itself held flashy lures along with other gear, Webb's lunch and a small first-aid kit. The anchor was a sandbag attached to a thin nylon rope—England had explained that a sandbag did not damage coral. Rising from the storage box was a red caution flag to make him visible out on the water.

Seated with his feet in adjustable footrests, Webb had been comfortable as he paddled. There was a retainer bracket on the side of the kayak for him to clamp the paddle to as he fished, and there was a rod holder directly in front of him holding the rod that England had rigged, waiting for Webb to make his first casts.

His grandfather gave a smile of satisfaction as Webb floated almost to the shore. David was holding a small black pouch with a waterproof zip seal.

"Looks like you figured out a few things," David said.

Webb had been going back and forth just off the shore, paddling and steering the kayak, while David went to the cottage to get something. The black pouch, Webb guessed.

"Except for why you don't seem too worried about sending me out for a fishing trip by myself," Webb said.

"You worried?" David asked.

"No."

"Then I'm not either." David sat on the soft sand, his sandals almost at the edge of the water, and it put them at eye level. Webb was only a few feet offshore, bobbing in the gentle waves. He was grateful he didn't have to crane his head upward to talk to his grandfather.

David continued, "Here's what I think. Parents sometimes baby their kids too much. They hover, making sure that the kid doesn't make any mistakes. How does that do the kid any good? Making mistakes is how you learn. And learning from your mistakes is how you get confidence. I always figured that unless a situation would put my child's life in danger, I was going to allow them as much freedom as possible. This is not a dangerous situation."

David swept his arms to indicate the flat waters. "The deepest point here is what, five feet?"

Webb nodded.

"If you had to, could you swim across these waters to the neighboring island?"

It was maybe a half mile across. Webb was a good swimmer.

Webb nodded again.

"The kayak has a GPS locator. You have a cell phone in a plastic bag, and you're wearing a life jacket. I think it would be disrespectful to treat you like you don't have enough common sense and life skills to be out on those waters by yourself. You're not a little boy anymore, so I'm not going to treat you like one."

"Thanks," Webb said.

"Respect is a two-way street," David said. "I'm a little disappointed you thought you needed to sneak out of the cottage last night without telling me."

Webb said, "I should have. I'm sorry."

He didn't expect David's grin.

"I'm proud of you for not making an excuse," David said. "A man does something wrong, he should own up to it. Not try to put the blame elsewhere."

A man. Webb liked hearing that.

"I trust you had a good reason for going out?" David asked.

"That girl," Webb said. "Kristie. She knocked on my window and wanted to go for a walk. So we did."

"Oy!" David said. "Moonlight walk. Nice. First kiss?"

"Kiss?" Webb shook his head. "Nothing like that. She's too perfect to ruin things by trying a kiss."

"Aah," David said. He gave a huge grin. "Remember I reserved the right to talk like a grandfather? Need to use it now. Remember to get to know someone for who they are, not how they look. I'm old enough to know it's the inside that matters a lot more than the outside. Still, when your heart goes pitter-patter, it's a wonderful thing."

"And maybe we don't need to talk about it," Webb said. "Okay?"

David smiled. "Okay." Then his expression turned serious. "Something else we don't have to talk about, but I'll be here for you if you need to bounce things off me."

David rose and waded two steps into the water and handed Webb the black pouch.

"I've been wondering when the best time might be to give this to you," David said. "And obviously, I've decided on this morning. I wanted you to be alone when you watched it."

Webb unzipped the pouch and looked inside to see an iPod.

"Um, thanks," Webb said. It seemed the polite thing to say. Webb already had a device, and this iPod wasn't the latest.

"This technology always amazes me," David said. "I remember when you needed huge reel-to-reel tapes and a projector the size of a sewing machine if you wanted to watch home movies."

"Was this before or after the airplane was invented?" Webb asked.

"Ha-ha," David said. Then the serious look returned to his face. "You don't talk much about your stepfather," he said.

"Not much to say," Webb said. "And whatever there is, it's kind of like the Kristie thing. I want to keep it to myself."

"Fair enough," David said. "So I'll say what I need to say, and you don't have to answer. My sense is that things could be better at home for you than they are. I'm here for you if you want to talk. And in the meantime, there's something on the iPod for you to watch. Something your father gave to me a few months before he died. He told me to only let you see it if I felt you needed to see it. He didn't want to get in the way of you and a relationship with a new father."

"This is from my dad? A video?"

"Your dad," David said. "When you watch it, you'll understand. And remember, I'm here if you want to discuss it."

Webb stared into the pouch.

His dad.

Webb's grandfather stepped out of the water.

"As you go around the key, stay within a couple hundred yards of shore, okay?" David said. "How about three hours? Be back by then. If you're not, I'll start calling your cell, and we'll search for you by GPS."

"Yeah," Webb said. But his mind was on the iPod in the small pouch.

His dad.

Webb paddled away from shore with a sensation like the iPod was a bomb set on a timer.

ELEVEN

The water was less than waist deep, and so clear that he could see the bone-white sandy bottom. The humid breeze seemed to soak into Webb's skin and muscles. He let out a deep sigh, thinking about the iPod.

His dad?

Seven years had passed since he'd said goodbye to his dad for the final time. Lots of nights Webb would dream that he was in the backyard, playing catch with his dad. It was such a plain, ordinary thing to be doing, and that's why he would wake up sad. Something so plain and ordinary wasn't ever going to be part of his life again. When he saw other kids with their dads, even doing things as ordinary as waiting in line for a burger or the dad reaching across the table to dip a fry into the kid's ketchup, Webb wanted to go over and tell the kid how lucky he was.

Lately Webb hadn't been having those kinds of dreams.

Webb decided to take his mind off the iPod. He grabbed the rod and threw the lure out as far as he could. It felt great, letting the leverage of the rod work like a giant arm to hurl the few ounces of metal a hundred yards away.

England had called it a topwater plug. It had a swivel in the center, and as Webb reeled it back to the kayak, the lure splashed from side to side just like an injured baitfish.

Webb didn't care whether he caught anything. It was just amazing to be sitting on clear water in the Florida Keys, enjoying the sensations of sun and breeze and the rhythm of reeling in the lure.

He wanted the enjoyment of the moment to keep him from thinking about his dad.

Webb cast and reeled a few times, letting the kayak drift in the water.

Without warning, a dark blotch the size of a kite showed up on the bone-white sand. It scooted forward, leaving a cloud of white particles expanding in the the water.

Stingray, Webb thought. Very cool.

He tossed out the lure again. But his thoughts kept returning to the iPod.

For years, Webb had loved those dreams of his dad. It was almost like his dad was finding a way to visit him. Lately, though, Webb had been thinking about his dad not with sadness but anger. Why had his dad left him so that a stepfather would enter Webb's life?

A video to him from his dad. He should have been excited, but he wasn't. There were days he felt like his dad had abandoned him. It was not a rational feeling. His dad obviously would not have wanted to die. But the feeling was there, and it made him resent his dad. He didn't know if he wanted his dad to talk to him from the dead. Webb had been so angry lately that he didn't want to play guitar. Rejecting guitar was like rejecting his dad.

Webb knew his grandfather had been hinting for Webb to tell him what was happening at home.

Not a chance.

Webb never wanted to push his stepfather past the point of irritation to the point of anger. Webb was afraid of his stepfather. He was afraid of what his stepfather might do if Webb told anyone what it was like at home. The problem was, Webb couldn't prove anything to anyone about his stepfather's cruelty. His stepfather had been in the military and knew all the tricks.

Webb had even set up a spy cam in his bedroom once, hoping it would capture something he could show to an outside authority—how his stepfather managed to make innocent comments seem like threats. Part of the trouble was how someone else might hear the words. Yes, innocent on the surface. But deep down, terrifying for someone who had to live in the house with his stepfather. And it wasn't just about protecting Webb; Webb needed to protect his mother.

The spy cam had not worked.

Webb's stepfather had found the spy cam and removed it without a word. Webb had come into his bedroom and it was gone. That had been more scary than if his stepfather had confronted him. Instead, Webb had waited for months for punishment, dreading every night alone in bed, waiting for the door to open. It probably served him right for setting something in his bedroom to spy on…

Huh.

Webb snapped out of those thoughts and stopped reeling in the lure.

Huh.

He closed his eyes, trying to picture the night table beside Jonathan Greene's bed.

Huh.

After using a remote control for the mattress, Greene had set the remote down on the bedside table. Beside that digital picture frame.

In researching spy cams to buy one for himself, Webb had learned that some recorders were hidden in digital picture frames. Called nanny cams. For parents who wanted to make sure that babysitters were not doing anything strange.

Webb rested his rod in the holder in front of him, with the lure now settled at the bottom of the water a long way out.

He half turned so he could reach the storage box behind him. His iPhone was in a waterproof case. He pulled it out and winced as bright sun reflected off the screen into his eyes.

Webb's grandfather had set Webb up with a roaming data package. Webb went to the device's browser and searched the Amazon site for "nanny cam."

There it was. He felt a sudden lurch of adrenaline when he saw the listing. He expanded the view. *Nanny Cam—Video Recorder Hidden In Digital Photo Frame. With Self Playback feature.*

He read more and grew certain that's what he'd seen at Greene's bedside. And now that he thought about it, a digital frame seemed out of place when Greene didn't appear to have any other technology in the house. So maybe there was truth in the letters. Maybe they weren't just the ramblings of a man in his final days of life. Someone was spying on Greene.

Webb decided that kayaking for the day was over. This was important enough to go back to tell his grandfather.

Webb grabbed the rod. He needed to reel in the line so he could paddle back to the resort cottage.

Bam.

It was like something had grabbed the end of the lure to try to yank the rod out of Webb's fingers, something with the force of a slamming door.

It stunned him, and it took him a moment to figure out what had happened. Then there was a huge splash and the line on the reel began to strip with a high-pitched *zing* sound.

Something had taken the lure. Something big. Something very big. Something so big it began to tow his kayak.

TWELVE

Webb was distracted for a moment by the roar of two huge helicopters sweeping over him from the southwest, headed northeast to the Atlantic side of the Keys. They were so low that he could see the pilots. The helicopters were clearly marked *Coast Guard* and painted white with distinctive red stripes at the nose, midsection and tail.

The distraction didn't last long. The choppers followed the curve of the horizon and were soon out of sight, and as the sounds faded into silence, Webb's total focus was on the tip of his fishing rod.

During the cruise along the highway, his grandfather had told him that the rod was crucial to reeling in a powerful fish. The technique, David had said, was to pull the tip of the rod toward the sky. As a lever, it would drag the fish the same distance closer to the boat as the tip of the rod covered while raising it. Then you would lower the tip of the rod and quickly reel in as much line as possible. It put the strain on the rod and away from the reel.

Whatever was on the other end had the muscle to make Webb's shoulders hurt. Each time he leaned back to raise the tip of the rod, it would bend almost in half, vibrating at the strain. Then he'd lower the tip and reel in the line.

Again and again.

At one point, the rod looked like it was going to snap in half.

He needed to use drag.

On the reel was a small button to adjust how much tension the reel could take. David had warned Webb not to put his thumb on the line where it wrapped around the reel. If a big fish went on a tear-away run, the friction of the line as it spun off the reel would burn the pad of Webb's thumb.

Webb adjusted the drag so that the fish could pull off line instead of breaking it or snapping the rod.

The way to win, David had told him, was to make it as difficult as possible for the fish to pull line off the reel but without letting the fish snap the fishing line. The way to win was to let the fish tire itself to the point of exhaustion.

With the drag set now so that Webb didn't risk losing the fish completely, he went back to raising the tip and reeling as he lowered it.

Each time he braced himself to lift the tip of the rod away from the water and the fish, it felt fractionally easier.

Yes, the fish was tiring. It was no longer pulling the kayak.

Webb managed to get the fish close enough for his first glimpse of the silvery torpedo. It seemed at least half the length of the kayak.

At the same time, the fish must have seen Webb's outline, because it had a burst of panicked energy. It rose in the air, trying to shake the hook loose, and when it spurted away with fishing line, it left behind a cloud of sand in the water, like dust in the air.

Wow.

Webb was patient.

He knew he'd win the battle as long as he didn't snap the line.

Raise, lower and reel. Raise, lower and reel.

Again the fish got within sight.

This time it was too tired to do much more than a half roll.

It should have been victory.

Except Webb felt like a dog chasing a car. What's the dog going to do once it actually catches a car?

Webb had an idea.

England had doubted Webb's chances of catching anything without help. Before launching Webb in the kayak, England had sneered and told

Webb that there were fishing pliers in the storage box, not that Webb would ever need them.

But theory, as David often said, was often different than practice.

In theory, Webb could use fishing pliers on the monstrous fish. In practice, he didn't know how it was done.

He had two choices. Cut the line and let the fish go free with a hook in its mouth. Or work the lure out so the fish could hunt for itself again when it recovered energy.

Webb decided he would do his best to help the fish. He didn't want a trophy for his bedroom wall. He did want a photo to remember the fish.

Webb used his free hand to get his iPhone ready and then shot some video. He didn't even know what kind of fish it was, other than big. His grandfather would be able to tell Webb.

With that finished, Webb half turned again and found the fish pliers in the storage box.

It looked simple enough.

Clamp the teeth of the plier on the hook and turn the hook sideways to release it from the fish's mouth.

The fish flailed a few times as Webb reeled it in the last few feet, but not with enough strength to cause much more than a ripple on the water.

That's what lulled Webb into his mistake.

THIRTEEN

He thought the fish was tired to the point of death.

Webb was holding the fishing rod with his left hand, using the tip of the rod to guide the fish alongside the kayak. With the plier in his right hand, he leaned down to get a firm grip on the hook. The fish's large unblinking eyes were black circles, its teeth jagged little triangles.

Webb squeezed the plier hard. The fish, he knew, was too big for him to lift out of the water. The best he could do was pull it up a few inches, and as he did that, he twisted the hook.

The fish leapt high with all of its remaining energy, shoving the upper half of its body across the side of the kayak and flopping for a few seconds. It happened too fast for Webb to react, and just as quickly, the fish fell back into the water. With a few flicks of its tail, it disappeared.

Webb noticed first that he was still holding the fishing lure in the teeth of the pliers in his right hand. That last huge spasm by the fish had torn the hook from its mouth.

Webb noticed second the rivulet of red running down his left wrist.

Webb noticed third the searing pain as he realized that the fish had slashed the soft flesh of his forearm with those jagged triangular teeth.

Nice, he thought. He'd just lost a fight to a fish.

He glanced at the shoreline. It looked like it might be a twenty-minute paddle to haul the kayak up on the shore near the cottage.

He was bleeding hard. It didn't seem like it could kill him, but it also didn't seem smart to paddle and cause his heart to pump faster and push out blood faster.

He raised his left hand above his shoulders, hoping that would slow the bleeding a little. With his right hand he pulled the first-aid kit out of the storage box behind him. He turned to face the front of the kayak again, feeling the warmth of the blood as it trickled down to his elbow before plopping in large drops on the kayak.

It didn't look like any of the adhesive bandage strips would cover the cut, which was a slash running the length of his forearm. There was a roll of adhesive tape.

Webb had to lower his left hand and use it to cut strips of tape. He dipped his arm into the water, thinking the salt water might prevent infection. Red rivulets faded as the blood dispersed. He wasn't worried about sharks catching a scent of his blood. The water was too shallow for sharks. He placed the strips of tape crossways on his forearm to pull the sides of the cut together. He wrapped his forearm with strips of gauze.

They began to turn red as they soaked up blood, but it was the best he could do.

He'd probably have to go to the emergency room for stitches, but he grinned as he paddled. If a guy had to have a scar, it was nice to have a story to go with it.

But when he landed the kayak, that story didn't seem worth telling. Because he found out that the helicopters he'd noticed right after hooking the fish had been headed out on a rescue mission. A boat had capsized in the Gulf Stream.

Yeah.

The boat that Webb and his grandfather had decided not to go on earlier that morning.

FOURTEEN

"Can you feel this?" The question came from Dr. Stones as she pinched the skin of Webb's forearm. She wore white, and she had faded red hair and a tired expression.

Webb's grandfather had not taken Webb to an emergency room at the hospital at Key West, a half hour or so down the highway. Instead, they'd gone across to Big Pine Key and found a walk-in clinic.

Webb had his arm on a table, and the physician was preparing to stitch his forearm. David sat in the corner, quite relaxed. A small radio in the corner played soft music.

"No," Webb said. "Not feeling anything."

"I'll get started then," Dr. Stones said. "Let me know if I need to give you more freezing."

Dr. Stones began to peel off the tape that Webb had put across the slash. "You did a pretty good job of first aid on yourself. Good thing you had a video. That's going to make a great story, getting attacked by a barracuda."

Webb nodded, trying not to show a grin of pride.

Barracuda. He'd landed a barracuda. Yes, it would make for an amazing story. Might even impress Kristie.

"You might not want to watch," Dr. Stones said. "I'm going to put in as many stitches as possible. I'll use fine thread, and with luck there won't be much of a scar."

"Actually," Webb said, as blood oozed from the slash, "I'm a little curious about this."

Dr. Stones had a J-shaped needle with nylon thread. Webb watched as she lifted skin and poked the needle through one side of the cut and then the other. It seemed no different than sewing clothing. Except that it looked like Dr. Stones had to push the needle hard to get through the skin. The point of the needle would make a little tent before coming through on the other side.

"Huh," Webb said. "I didn't know skin was that tough."

"It's an amazing organ," she said. "Waterproof and self healing. Breathes and sweats. Drives me crazy when people don't take care of their skin with sunscreen. Or if they abuse it by smoking."

Dr. Stones looked over at David. "How old are you?"

"Old enough," he answered with a grin. "But young enough too, if you're looking for a walk along the bay."

"Ewww," Webb said. "Really? In front of me?"

Dr. Stones laughed.

"Well," she said to David, "whatever age I would guess probably isn't close to your actual age. You obviously exercise and eat healthy. Your skin is glowing, and you should be proud of it."

"More proud of my grandson here," David said. "I like how he didn't panic out on the water. But it proves my point. We don't have to baby our kids. We—"

Whatever else David was going to say was interrupted by a voice from the radio.

"News update," the voice said. "The US Coast Guard has reported the successful rescue of all people on board the pleasure craft that sank earlier today in the Gulf Stream a few miles offshore of Marathon. Credit is given to the fishing guide who made sure all were wearing life vests. Still no word on what caused the boat to capsize."

The radio returned to soft music.

"That was one of Jonathon Greene's boats," Dr. Stones said. "Didn't you say you were here to visit him?"

Webb nodded.

She sighed. "I hear things aren't going great for him healthwise."

"He doesn't have long," David said. "But he's not feeling sorry for himself. It's what happens.

We live. We die. It's what you do in between that matters."

"Amen," Dr. Stones said. She popped the needle through another piece of Webb's skin. "It's why I became a doctor. To do something meaningful during the in-between."

"My grandson here thinks death is contagious," David said.

Webb lifted his eyes to his grandfather, who didn't look away.

"Greene is in his last hours," David said to Webb. "He's got no family. I know you don't want to be there, but it's only uncomfortable if you want to pretend it's not happening."

David spoke to Dr. Stones. "It's not Webb's fault. That's another part of babying kids. We hide death from them, try to pretend it doesn't exist. Funeral homes are a billion-dollar business trying to shield us from reality. Bodies age and face the unexpected, like cancer. Death is part of life."

Webb flinched.

Dr. Stones said, "That last stitch hurt?"

Webb shook his head. He had flinched because of how his gut tightened with memories of his own dad in the hospital. He was getting angry at his grandfather, but this was not the place to express it. Actually, Webb thought, there was no time or place he wanted to share his feelings about his dad.

"It'll be my turn soon enough," David said. Although his grandfather was speaking to Dr. Stones, Webb knew that David wanted him to hear it and was using Dr. Stones to speak to him. "I've had a great life, but I still have some things I'd like to do, and I hope it can happen."

"Bucket list," Dr. Stones said. "Let your grandson help. Or grandsons. Didn't you say you have six?"

"Not a bad idea," David said. "A bucket list to finish all the things I want to do. In the meantime, I'm enjoying as much time as I can with my grandsons."

What Webb wanted to say was that maybe one of his grandsons wasn't enjoying it as much in return. Maybe one of his grandsons didn't like someone trying to teach him life lessons. Maybe one of his grandsons didn't want to talk about a dad or a stepfather. But when Webb was angry, he bottled it.

So Webb took a deep breath and watched in silence as Dr. Stones finished the stitches.

FIFTEEN

When Webb and his grandfather sat on their chairs at Jonathan Greene's bedside, the man seemed different than when Webb had first met him.

Greene's face was more hollowed, but the skin seemed tighter. His eyes weren't clouded, but piercing. His wheezing had disappeared.

"I'm ready," Greene said. "I wish it was different, but I'm ready. I just need to tell you something first."

He reached out and clutched at David's forearm as a spasm went through him.

"I did something," Greene said. "I was just a boy. Same age as your grandson now. Boys should be forgiven if they make mistakes?"

"Boys or men," David said. "If they try to make it right."

"It was the hurricane," Greene said. "The big one. Nineteen thirty-five."

"Nineteen thirty-five," David said softly.

"Nineteen thirty-five," Greene said. "I was born in '22. Makes me thirteen when it happened. Just a couple weeks after my birthday. You can't ever know what it was like. Dark. Rain. Wind. Waves. Monster waves blowing across the Keys. People tied themselves to trees just to survive. And the train. The locomotive. The wind just tore it off the tracks. Tore out the tracks. Entire bridges moved. It was the end of the railroad, and we didn't know it until the next morning. The group of men the train was supposed to take back to the mainland? None of them made it."

Greene shifted his eyes to Webb. "A person always knows the right thing to do. Because it's always the most difficult choice. Learn it now, not after it's too late."

Tears trickled down Greene's cheek.

In that moment a new feeling hit Webb. Compassion. He'd been seeing Greene as a withered old man, not as a real person. A dying man to be pitied and feared. But seeing Greene so vulnerable and open, so in need of understanding…that's what cracked Webb apart.

It also gave Webb a sense of shame. His grandfather, from the moment they'd first seen Greene, had related to him as one human to another. Webb had been so wrapped up in himself, he hadn't looked beyond to see that someone else needed help.

Webb took a tissue and gently wiped some spittle off Greene's face. His fingers trembled. He wished in that moment that he could have done the same for his own dad when his dad was in the hospital.

"The next day," Greene said, "we went out in rescue teams. Wreckage everywhere. We had dogs to help us find bodies. We listened for survivors. That locomotive was on its side in the water. Parts of the Keys had disappeared. Other parts were new. Channels were gone, new channels cut. It's the most famous storm in Key history, and trust me, there was a good reason for it. The railroad was destroyed and never rebuilt."

Greene closed his eyes and let out a long breath. His chest rose and fell in a slower rhythm. He spoke with his eyes closed.

"I was the one who found him. I knew who he was. His picture had been in the newspapers. He was a mobster. Rumrunner. Prohibition had ended, but everyone knew how he had made his fortune. He was under a big piece of lumber. A train tie that had been torn loose. He was weak. I think his ribs were broken. He couldn't move the lumber himself. He had blood all across his face, covering his eyes. He couldn't see me, but he could hear me."

When Greene opened his eyes again, he stared at the ceiling. It was as if he was alone, speaking to himself. "There was a satchel nearby. He promised me I could have it if I helped him. There were…"

Greene took a deep breath. "There were wads of hundred-dollar bills inside. Diamonds too. A man like that—he didn't come by that kind of money honestly. I knew that as soon as a man like was all healed up, he'd come and take it away. Even if I hid it, he'd do something to get it back. What I decided to do was run with the satchel and put it in a safe place, then come back and pretend I had just found him and that the satchel had never been there in the first place."

Greene groaned. "What I forgot about was the tide. I hid that satchel in some mangroves, and when I came back, the water was over his head. My fault. And that money—how could I tell people where it came from? Even if I lied and said I found it somewhere else, someone would find a way to take it from me. So I kept that satchel hidden for a long time, and later, after the war, I told people I made the money during the war, and then I used it to buy land. This big house? It's mine because I let a man die. And now it's my turn to die. If I could go back, I'd do it differently so I'd never close my eyes at night and see the water above that man's face, waving his hair so gentle…"

David patted the man's hand.

"Maybe leaving everything I have to that charity will make a difference," Greene said. "It's the best I can do. Those diamonds. Did you find them? They're worth a lot of money. That can really help the kids in the charity."

"The diamonds," David said. "We—"

Greene let out a gasp. His chest stilled. It didn't rise again.

"He's dead," Webb whispered. "Dead."

David put his arm around Webb's shoulders. "Sometimes dying is easier than living."

SIXTEEN

Two hours later, Webb sat with his grandfather on the patio outside their cottage. It was a warm, cloudless night, and the moon was visible through the leaves of the palmetto trees. The buzz of insects made for a comforting blanket of background noise.

"I'm tired but not sleepy," David said. "You?"

"Tired but not sleepy," Webb said.

Paramedics had arrived within minutes of the 9-1-1 call. They had confirmed time of death. Webb and his grandfather had been asked to wait until police arrived and had been told that was standard procedure. They had waited in the dining room until police confirmed that the death was not suspicious and then waited until someone from a local funeral home arrived to handle the body.

"How do you feel?" David asked.

"Tired but not sleepy."

"That's a way to avoid my question, right?"

"Right," Webb said.

"Not one to discuss your feelings."

"Answering that would require discussing feelings," Webb said.

"That's why you haven't talked about the video from your dad?" David asked.

"I haven't watched it," Webb said. "There was the barracuda, then the cut on my arm, then the trip to the medical clinic, then the visit to Greene and then the rest of the evening."

"If you're tired but not sleepy," David said, "I'd suggest a walk to watch it. It's important to hear what your dad has to say. Otherwise I wouldn't have asked. Because I'm not sure you've ever had a chance to deal with his death."

That's when it hit Webb. Of the six grand-sons, his grandfather had chosen Webb for a trip to Florida to sit at a dying man's bedside. Because David wanted Webb to talk about his own dad.

No way, Webb thought. He wouldn't talk about that with anyone.

Webb tried to swallow his anger at his grand-father and said, "Are you curious about the nanny cam?"

The moonlight cutting through the palmetto leaves gave his grandfather's face a ghostly appear-ance and softened the older man's expression. Still, Webb could see that his grandfather was debating whether to push Webb about his father. As the silence continued, Webb was okay with not trying to fill it.

Then David said, "While your stubbornness makes me want to bang my head against a wall,

I admire and respect it. Last chance. Want to talk about your father?"

Webb said, "Are you curious about the nanny cam?"

His grandfather gave a theatrical sigh. "I am curious about the nanny cam."

"While we were waiting for the police," Webb said, "I went to the bathroom down the hall. It took less than a minute to figure out how it works. And yes, it's set up to record conversations."

"To confirm," David said. "Someone leaves the nanny cam there. Lets it pick up conversations. Then picks up the camera later?"

"I can't see how it was set up to send out recordings wirelessly."

"So whoever did this needed to be able to come in and out on a regular basis?"

"Yes," Webb said. "Maybe had a couple of identical nanny cams and switched them out."

"Leading to another question. Why? And I think I can answer that. If Greene was babbling things because of his painkillers, that person was hoping to learn something from the babbling, right?"

"Like where Greene might have some money hidden?" Webb asked. "Or the diamonds?"

"Yes," David answered. "Which tells us something else about the person who put the nanny cam there. He knew enough about Greene to suspect there was a secret. That would mean someone close to Greene."

"Or she," Webb said.

"Greene's live-in nurse?"

"That's the obvious guess," Webb said. "Plus, while I was in the bathroom I replayed one of the recordings. Just enough to know that we should give it a good listen."

"Well then," David said, "why don't we?"

Webb found the almost hidden switch on the back of the frame that played back audio, and they both leaned forward to listen.

SEVENTEEN

It was the nurse's voice. Yvonne Delta. And Greene's voice. Webb easily pictured the words as if they had been transcribed.

Delta: I want to make you more comfortable. Is there anything I can do?

Greene: Stop coming to me with questions. I have given you enough already. I don't owe you more. I have nothing left to say.

Delta: You are lying to me. Last night, in your sleep, you talked about it again. The diamonds. Where are the diamonds?

Greene: Woman, I put the money in the bank years ago. After the war. You know that. Everybody knows that.

Delta: There is more.

Greene: More?

Delta: The diamonds. You talked about diamonds.

Greene: No. No diamonds!

Delta: You're lying to me. You still have diamonds from that man. The man you drowned.

Greene: I…did…not…drown him.

Delta: You let him die. That is the same. You ran with his money and his diamonds and you let him die.

Greene: Please. Let me die in peace. After all that you have bled from me, at least give me that in return.

Delta: Where are the diamonds? When you babble, you talk about diamonds in different places.

Greene: No diamonds.

Delta: That is not what you say in your dreams. I've looked where you first said they were. But that's not the place. Where are they hidden?

Greene: I am so tired.

Delta: Where are they hidden?

[silence]

Delta: Jonathan?

[silence]

Delta: Jonathan?

[silence]

Webb clicked off the switch and set the picture frame down. He became aware again of the buzzing of the night insects.

"Huh," David said.

"Hysterical reactions like that don't help anybody," Webb said.

David snorted at Webb's sarcasm. "You and me, we don't like showing a lot of what we're thinking."

"Don't even like talking about how we don't like showing what we're feeling," Webb said.

"How about talking about Yvonne instead? There was a lot in that conversation."

"She's been blackmailing him, it sounds like," David said. "For years. So she knew he'd let a man die and took advantage of it."

"It also sounds like she believes the diamonds exist," Webb said.

David shrugged. "Wouldn't surprise me if they had been there once. Do you know what Prohibition was?"

"No."

"Don't hold me to getting the dates exactly right," David said, "but a little less than a hundred years ago, the government made it illegal to make or sell any kind of alcohol. Fortunes were made by people willing to smuggle it into the United States. They were called rum-runners. When Prohibition ended in the 1930s, rumrunners could build those fortunes in other illegal ways. They dealt in cash. Diamonds too, I guess. Much easier to carry diamonds than gold."

"But maybe not so easy to bring diamonds into a bank and make a deposit."

"That would be my guess. We know that Jonathan waited until after the war to put that money in the bank, telling everybody he earned it during the war. I wouldn't be surprised if he kept the diamonds hidden."

"And then talked about it because of the painkillers."

"I don't think it was an accident that Yvonne was his housekeeper," David said. "And I think we'll need to talk to her."

"Tonight?" Webb asked.

"Tomorrow," his grandfather answered. "Tonight I'm asking you as your grandfather to do that one thing for me. Go listen to what your dad wanted you to hear."

Webb gave his grandfather a questioning look.

"Many times in his last months, he told me that he wanted you to have a great father," David said. "He was hoping your mom would eventually remarry and that your stepdad would be everything that he had wanted to be for you. He made the video to be able to talk to you if that didn't happen. He asked me not to show it to you if you had a great stepfather, because he didn't want to get between you and that person. But he asked that if someday I felt you needed to see the videos…"

David took a deep breath. "You won't talk about it, but I know what you have at home isn't the father he wanted for you. So why don't you give your dad a chance to be that father? He made more than a few videos, talking to you as if the two of you were sitting on a porch. Advice and questions. Just listen, okay? If you like this first video, I'll get you the others."

EIGHTEEN

Webb thought he was alone, but he was wrong.

He sat on the trunk of a long, fallen mangrove, with his sandaled feet on the sand. The breeze felt good across his face. He had the iPod in his hand, and he was working up the courage to view the video.

"Hey," came Kristie's voice, soft in the night air.

Webb slid the iPod into his pocket as he stood and turned.

She was almost at the mangrove trunk.

"Hope I didn't make you jump," Kristie said.

"Hey," Webb said. "Nice to see you."

"I was on my usual walk," she said. "I saw you leaving the cottage and I followed. Is that okay?"

She didn't wait for Webb's answer. She moved to the mangrove trunk and sat on it. She grabbed Webb's arm and pulled him down so that he was sitting beside her. She leaned her shoulder against Webb's shoulder, and he caught the trace of perfume in the air.

Wow, he thought. This feels so good.

"I heard about Jonathan Greene," she said. "I heard you were there. That must have been horrible."

That's what Webb would have thought if someone had told him ahead of time that he would be with a person when that person died. Except it hadn't turned out like that. He'd learned that dying was part of living.

"I think," Webb said, "he was glad not to be alone."

That, Webb realized, would be the hardest part. Not to have someone nearby, especially if you were afraid or if you weren't ready. It made him think of his dad. Webb didn't even know if someone had been right there when his dad died. Had his mom been there at that moment, or had he been alone? He would ask his grandfather.

"Was Greene talking or anything?" Kristie asked.

"Anything?"

"People say he had treasure hidden somewhere in the Keys. It would be so cool if you found out something about it. You know, deathbed confession."

"Oh," Webb said. "That kind of anything. I guess if you hadn't been there, something like that does sound cool. But you know, it seems kind of sacred, when someone moves from life into death. It's not something you want to make into a campfire story, if you've been there."

"So he didn't give out any big secrets?"

Webb felt a tiny barb of irritation. Hadn't he just said it wasn't the kind of thing to turn into a story? Wasn't she listening? Maybe she didn't understand, because she hadn't been there.

What a huge realization, in your final moments, to know that the journey of life was going to end. It was the kind of realization where you would want to know that you had lived your life as well as you could, and the kind of realization where you would hope you didn't have any big regrets.

Then it stabbed Webb, the thought of what his dad might have been thinking in those final moments in the hospital. All these years Webb had been focused only on himself, getting angrier and angrier about the fact that his father had died and left him alone, so that someday a stepfather would step into the situation and home would become a place that wasn't even close to a home.

An image flashed into Webb's head. Of his dad in that hospital bed, opening his eyes at night in a room that had that horrible hospital smell, of his dad feeling his life slipping away, of his dad thinking about a little boy he'd leave behind and of his dad regretting that he couldn't spend any more time with his little boy.

Webb felt a choking sensation in his throat. It took him a second to realize what it was.

"Got to go," Webb said. His voice felt hoarse.

"Stay," she said. She reached for his hand.

He waved it away. "Got to go."

He stumbled away from the fallen mangrove. The choking in his throat became a sob. He hoped she couldn't hear.

He was a hundred yards down the waterline when that sob became a heaving motion in his throat, and the tears in his eyes nearly blinded him as he began to bawl in anguish, thinking about all that his dad had faced in those final days and final minutes.

All Webb could say were three words, over and over again.

"I'm sorry, Dad. I'm sorry, Dad. I'm sorry, Dad."

When he'd cried himself out alone in the moonlight, Webb reached into his pocket for the iPod and started the video.

His father's face appeared on the screen.

"Hey, little cowboy," his dad said with a smile, "I sure love you."

Webb began to sob again.

NINETEEN

Yvonne Delta lived in a small square house across the water on Big Pine Key, a few blocks away from the main commercial strip where Webb had visited the medical clinic the day before. The skin on Webb's forearm felt tight, but it didn't throb. That, David told him, was an excellent sign that the cut was not infected.

Webb had left his grandfather at the outdoor patio of a coffee shop just down from the medical clinic. They had agreed that Yvonne would feel less threatened by a kid Webb's age than by David and maybe tell Webb more things than she might tell David.

The address had been easy to find—she was listed in the phone book. Webb had enjoyed teasing his grandfather about how ancient that kind of technology was; after all, who actually picked up paper when you could jump on your device and find the information on the Internet?

On the sidewalk in front of Yvonne's house, Webb pulled out his phone and called David, who answered immediately.

"All good?" David asked.

"All good," Webb said. "I'm ready to knock on her door."

"I'll be here," David said.

Nothing else needed to be said. They'd already talked about how Webb might begin his questions. Webb didn't hang up on the conversation. Instead, he slipped the phone into the front pocket of his shirt and left the connection open. David would be listening to every word.

Webb followed a sidewalk into the front yard of Yvonne's house, which had a neatly trimmed lawn and huge shade trees. The house had been recently painted and had flower planters on the front steps. But even with the shade of trees in the front yard, Webb felt the heat from the midmorning sun. It had been worse on the sidewalk, with the glare of the sun bouncing off concrete as he walked the few blocks from the café to her house.

Webb felt sweat on his skin, and he was glad he'd worn a loose shirt. At least the sweat wasn't showing up in huge wet spots on the fabric.

He rang the doorbell. He heard approaching footsteps, and then the peephole in the door darkened, so he knew she was looking at him.

"I'm Jim Webb," he said to the door. "My grandfather was a friend of Jonathan Greene's. Remember? We just visited, and you let us into the house a few nights ago. Could I talk to you about something Mr. Greene told us before he died?"

The door opened. A waft of cool air hit Webb from the interior as he got his first really good look at Yvonne Delta. She was probably twenty years younger than his own grandfather. She was fighting off the years with dark dyed hair. Webb thought that exercise and a sense of fashion might be a better approach, because she was lumpy and in a drab dress. His grandfather, on the other hand, seemed much more vigorous and healthy and took pains to dress with style, so it didn't matter that his hair was nearly white.

"I suppose you should come in," Yvonne said. "Air-conditioning is expensive, and I need to shut the door."

"Thank you," Webb said.

She pointed him to a chair in the small living room. The furniture was worn and plain. Paintings of animals in natural settings hung on the walls. Webb didn't see any family photographs.

Webb pulled the digital photo frame out from inside his shirt and set it on the coffee table in front of him. He watched carefully to see how Yvonne would react.

"Don't need to see any of his photos," she said. "He's gone and I'm not interested in his life."

Cold, he thought.

"It seemed like you wanted to avoid me and my grandfather during our visits," Webb said. "Is there a reason why?"

"What a rude question," she answered. "My life is none of your business. You said you wanted to talk about Jonathan Greene."

Webb picked up the frame again. "He had some secrets, didn't he?"

"Everyone does," she snapped. "And I already told you I'm not interested in photos."

Webb was puzzled. He and David had thought the sight of the nanny cam would be a powerful threat to get her to talk. He put it down again.

"My grandfather asked some questions about you," Webb told her. "We found out that your father was great friends with Jonathan Greene. They fought in World War Two together.

Your father returned to the Keys to become a banker. Greene started his business here."

"Common knowledge," Yvonne said. "For this, you're wasting my time?"

"What if your father told you some secrets about Greene?" Webb said. "Like how Greene really got his money. And what if you made sure you started working for Greene so you could begin to blackmail him? And then you heard him talking about diamonds because of painkillers?"

TWENTY

For a moment Yvonne's face went slack with surprise. Then she said, "You'd be a fool to believe what a dying old man might have told you."

It was obvious, though, that his words had shaken her.

Webb shrugged and picked up the nanny cam again. "You're not worried about this?"

"Photos?" She snorted. "Oh no. Please put it away. I'm so terrified of how they'll bore me."

Then she stood and said, "If you don't leave now, I'll call the police."

This meant he needed to use the blunt approach he and his grandfather had decided stood the best chance of working.

Webb said, "Sure. Let's call the police. Then you can explain to them about this photo frame and how you tried to record everything he said while he was delirious."

"You're a very confused boy," she said. "And whatever you think you are doing by threatening me with photos won't matter. The police are going to believe me over you any day."

"How about I make my own call? To the IRS."

"Internal Revenue Service?" she said. She sat again.

Webb would never have thought of this approach. It had been David's idea. Webb hoped David was hearing every word through the open cell-phone connection.

"I think blackmail would not be hard to prove," Webb told Yvonne. "How many years did he give you money to keep quiet about what happened after the hurricane? Since you started working for him?"

"Fairy tales," Yvonne said. "Good luck convincing people of that."

Webb said, "There's something called the Whistleblower Informant Award."

He and David had looked it up on the IRS website.

"Let me see if I've memorized it right," Webb said. He paused. "The IRS may pay awards to people who provide specific and credible information to the IRS if the information results in the collection of taxes, penalties, interest or other amounts from the noncompliant taxpayer."

Webb took a breath and tilted his head like he was thinking. A moment later he said, "Yup, that's about right. But don't take my word for it. Look it up on the IRS website. Any money you made as a blackmailer would make you a noncompliant taxpayer. Unless you reported it as income."

"Nothing can be proven."

"Maybe not the blackmail part. But I'm pretty sure the income part can. They would match money he took out of his bank to money you put into yours. But I'd rather not have to report you."

She looked at him with disbelief. "You're trying to blackmail me?"

Webb gave her another shrug. He thought of playing the recording on the nanny cam, but if the sight of the digital photo frame didn't scare her, the recording wouldn't. It seemed strange, that.

"What do you want?" she asked.

Webb said only two words. "The truth."

She laughed. "I'll be happy to tell the truth. Jonathan Greene became a murderer when he was a boy. He used the money he made from that murder to build his business here in the Keys. Get a newspaper reporter, and I'll tell him or her everything."

"What do you want me to tell the IRS?"

"Anything you want," she said. "All they will find out is that I was paid a nice high salary to be his nurse for the last few years. A very high salary." She smiled. "I'm not an idiot. I reported all my income. No matter where it came from."

Webb had thought this would be a moment of triumph. But it seemed the opposite.

She stood one more time. "So. Are you going to leave? Or do I call the police to make you leave?"

Webb left. Confused.

TWENTY-ONE

"Hey," Kristie said to Webb. "Great to see you."

Webb had received a text message from Kristie asking him if he wanted to go for a walk along the water. With the sunset putting an orange glow on the water, she'd been waiting for him in the public parking lot, sitting on the hood of a Jeep like she owned it.

"Great to see you too," Webb said. "Better than killing time at the cottage."

"I don't have long for a walk," Kristie said. "I have to be onstage in about an hour."

She gave him a smile. "And you haven't forgotten about tomorrow night, right? Battle of the Bands? I'll need you in the crowd, cheering for me."

"Haven't forgotten," Webb said. But it seemed like she'd forgotten that he'd been prepared to play guitar a few evenings ago until Sylas had made him leave. But then, she was the star. He was just someone who was supposed to cheer for her.

"Great," she said. "Let's go for a walk."

She jumped down from the Jeep hood and landed awkwardly. "Ouch." She reached down and rubbed her ankle. "Stupid sandals."

Webb's eyes followed her hand, and he noticed something on the pavement beside her sandal. A smeared cigarette butt. In a circle about the twice the size of a quarter. A swirl of blackened tobacco. He'd seen that same swirl before.

"Come on," Kristie said, taking Webb's hand.

Girl. Water's edge. Evening as the stars came out. It should have been another *wow* moment for Webb. Yet he couldn't help but think about the swirl of tobacco. It made him wonder if she would start asking certain types of questions. The same questions she asked every time they got together.

"How much longer are you staying down here?" Kristie asked.

"Not long enough," Webb said. "It's going to be tough to leave the sun and the water to head back north."

"I've heard Canada is beautiful," she said.

"It is," he answered. "But a person can get tired of snow."

"Trust me," she said, "a person can get tired of sun and heat. The trick is to go back and forth, I guess."

He wanted to enjoy what it felt like to hold hands with her.

"I guess," he said.

"But that would take money," she said. "Lots of it."

"It sure would," he said.

"Like, what if you could find a bunch of it," she said. "Like if the stories about Jonathan Greene were true. That would be so cool. Like if he had told your grandfather about where it was hidden. You know, before he died."

There it was. She hadn't asked anything, but still it was like a question. This time he was ready.

Webb said, "Actually, he did."

"What?" Kristie stopped and faced him. She moved in a little on the space between them. Her eyes were wide-open and she spoke breathlessly, with her lips parted as if she were about to kiss Webb.

It should have been another *wow* moment. Like maybe it would become his first kiss. Near the water. At sunset.

But he wasn't seeing how pretty her face was. He was seeing a swirl of blackened tobacco. Like maybe she'd been talking to someone else before he showed up. Someone who liked putting out hand-rolled cigarettes by stomping them with his heel and giving them a twist.

"Don't tell anybody," Webb said, "but I know exactly where it is. A second box of diamonds. The first box is gone. But he told us about another box. Nobody else knows except me and my grandfather. But my grandfather didn't believe what Greene told him because the first box was gone. I do. I think there is a second box. And tomorrow I'm going to go get it."

"No way!" Kristie said. "Where?"

"I'm going to pretend I'm headed off fishing in the kayak. Then, if what Jonathan Greene told my grandfather was true, I'll be back with a pouch full of diamonds."

"You are amazing!" Kristie said. She moved forward and stood on her toes and kissed Webb on the cheek.

She stepped back and smiled at him.

Even though it was only on the cheek, it was officially his first kiss. Webb knew he'd remember it for a long, long time.

TWENTY-TWO

Webb and his grandfather believed they had found the perfect spot for a double ambush.

First, it was a few hundred yards away from US Route 1, on the west side of Little Torch Key. This was important. The highway followed the route of the original Flagler railroad, which had been destroyed by the hurricane of 1935. It would seem believable that all those years earlier, when Jonathan Greene had been a boy involved in a rescue operation after the railroad was destroyed, he would not have gone too far when he took the satchel from the mobster and hid some diamonds.

Second, the location was reachable by road. Webb had kayaked from the resort on the east end, south around the tip of the key and then back up the west side. By car, David had been able to drive to near the spot, taking with him mosquito netting and two folding chairs and bottles of drinking water.

Third, the vegetation along the shoreline made it easy to watch the kayak and remain hidden under the mosquito netting. Webb had anchored the kayak and waded to shore.

Fourth, the water was too shallow for a motorboat to swoop in. If someone was going to get close, they'd be restricted to kayak speed.

All of this made it perfect for their ambush. Now they were expecting one in return.

As for the other ambush, the kayak was just offshore, screened by overhanging branches of mangrove trees. Better yet, if someone was going to ambush the kayak, it was hidden from the highway and was easy for anyone to sneak up on. That made it a perfect ambush target.

If Webb's guess was right, that would happen sometime in the next hour or two.

They'd added one more detail.

A dummy.

It had not been difficult to make a trip over to Big Pine Key and buy one from a secondhand clothing store. The dummy was about Webb's size. After Webb had anchored the kayak, they had dressed it in the clothes Webb was wearing when he paddled away from the resort. Long-sleeved striped shirt, bright-red shorts and a distinctive orange ballcap. Webb was now in comfortable brown shorts and a brown T-shirt, the better to blend in with the mosquito netting.

With the kayak nestled under the branches, someone would need to be within a few dozen feet of it to see that the "person" in it was a dummy. That would be close enough for David to film whoever came up to the kayak after tracking its location with GPS.

Webb had a good guess who it might be but needed to prove it.

He was settled in his chair, his grandfather in the other. David had the video camera in his lap. Webb had his iPhone ready to take video as backup. The mosquito netting was tented over them, supported by a couple of sticks that David had jammed into the sandy soil.

Both of them stared at the kayak.

Everything was ready. Now it was just a matter of waiting.

"This is sneaky," Webb said in a voice not much louder than a whisper.

"I'll take that as a compliment." It had been his grandfather's idea to set up the dummy. No way, he'd sternly said, was he going to put Webb at risk in any way.

"And if your hunch turns out to be correct," David continued in an equally soft voice, "you get the same compliment for telling Kristie last night that you would be headed out for diamonds this morning. That was truly sneaky."

"Hey, Grandpa," Webb said. "Your sneakiness is at a much higher level."

Yeah, *Grandpa*. Webb had said it. Felt good, letting some walls down.

"Hmm," David said. "Sneakiness? That almost sounds like an accusation."

Webb was glad his grandfather hadn't made a big deal about Webb not calling him David anymore. One thing to finally call him Grandpa, but no need to have a discussion about feelings.

"You could have made this trip to Florida by yourself," Webb said. "Jonathan Greene asked for your help, not our help. It could have been a two- or three-day trip, and you would have had lots of time for a different trip somewhere else with me."

"That does sound like an accusation."

"I don't think it's a coincidence that you gave me a video from my dad on the same trip where you brought me to be with your friend as he died, right?"

"Tell me this," David said. "Do you understand more about death than you did before? How angry have you been at your father? And how angry are you now?"

"Your questions answer my question," Webb said. "Can I just say thank you and leave it at that?"

His grandfather snorted. "I hate it when you gush. It's so awkward."

Webb thought of how he'd bawled and bawled after watching the video from his dad. He wouldn't be able to express to his grandfather how important that had been and how much it had changed things for Webb. Although his dad was gone, it was like he'd gotten him back.

"Yeah," Webb said. "Awkward. But really. Thanks, Grandpa. And when we get back, I'd love to see the other videos."

There was no chance for silence to settle back on them. Webb tapped his grandfather's knee and pointed.

A small upright pipe seemed to be drifting along the surface of the water toward them. As it got closer, it looked like it was dragging an alligator-like shadow.

Then Webb understood.

"Snorkeler," Webb said to his grandfather.

David had the video camera up and was catching the stealthy movement. Webb readied the camera on his iPhone.

They kept watching as the snorkeler moved to within yards of the kayak. Webb felt short of air and realized he hadn't breathed. He gently inhaled, keeping his hands steady as he kept the snorkeler in his viewfinder. He had his suspicions about the identity of the snorkeler, but so far all he could see was a man's body, flowing smoothly underwater.

Then, barely a matter of feet from the kayak, the man erupted out of the water and in one motion lifted a spear gun.

Webb bit back a gasp.

With a dull snap, the snorkeler fired the spear gun at the dummy in the kayak.

The thud of impact was equally dull, but the impact was devastating. The spear hit the dummy in the left shoulder, spinning it in a half circle and flinging the ballcap from the dummy's head onto a branch.

For a moment the snorkeler froze. And in the next moment obviously comprehended that this had been a trap. He dropped the spear gun, sank back into the water and began to swim away, roiling the water with each powerful kick of his flippers.

TWENTY-THREE

"Did you get that?" Webb half-shouted to his grandfather. He couldn't keep the excitement out of his voice as he leapt from the chair and cast away the mosquito netting.

"Yes!"

Webb brought up his own video coverage on the iPhone to make sure he hadn't missed it. He clicked *Play*. It was there. The rising snorkeler. The raised spear gun. The spear hitting the dummy.

What wasn't there was a clear identification of the snorkeler. With water streaming from the snorkeler's face mask, Webb couldn't be sure it was who he suspected it might be.

Webb was angry. More than angry. It was heated rage.

If he had been in the kayak instead of that dummy, the spear would be deep inside his back, and he'd be lying in agony among the roots of the mangroves. Or dead.

Webb threw his iPhone into the pocket of his shorts and scrambled forward toward the dummy.

"Webby," his grandfather called. "You need to stay."

Not a chance. Webb wasn't going to ask for permission. Not with the chance that his grandfather would try to hold him back. This was a time for action, not debate.

He let his rage give him extra fuel to burst through the mangroves to the dummy.

It was on its side. The force of the arrow had completely pierced it. That only added to Webb's rage, as again he realized that it could have been him.

Webb took a step into the water. He grabbed the spear gun where it was settling into the sand a few feet beneath the clear surface.

"No!" his grandfather yelled. "Just the kayak. That was our plan. Just the kayak."

Webb pretended not to hear. He was good at that.

Webb flipped the dummy's torso from the kayak, then yanked the spear from the dummy. He slammed the kayak back into the water.

"Don't!" his grandfather yelled. "He's the monster. Not you."

Webb was already in the kayak. He placed the spear gun across his lap and positioned the spear along the length of the paddle. Now he could paddle and hold the spear at the same time.

"Webby!" His grandfather had splashed into the water. "You don't know what you'll bring on yourself. Leave the spear gun!"

Webb didn't look back, didn't acknowledge that he could hear his grandfather.

The snorkeler was out in the bay and making the turn around the small point of land, heading back toward the bridge that carried the highway from key to key, the same bridge that had once held a railroad track and been torn apart by a hurricane.

Webb paddled hard and efficiently, quickly gaining on the snorkeler. Now it was a race, but Webb knew he was going to win.

He dug in with the paddle and gained on the snorkeler. But he needed time to do more than just win the race. He needed to be able to stop and load the spear gun.

As he paddled, he glanced down again and again at the gun on his lap, trying to figure out how it worked.

He could see that it was just a barrel with a trigger mechanism on the handle. The wooden barrel had a groove in it for the spear. At the other end of the barrel there was a thick rubber band in the shape of a horseshoe. It was obvious that all he needed to do was lay the spear into the groove, fit the pulling end of the rubber band over the back end of the spear and pull the band back far enough to lock the top of the trigger mechanism.

He gave a few hard thrusts with the paddle and let the kayak's momentum keep him going forward as he armed the spear gun. Then he set it across his lap and surged forward again.

He caught up to the snorkeler about a hundred yards from the boat that was waiting.

Now what?

For a moment—and only a moment—he saw the image of the snorkeler firing a spear into the dummy that was supposed to be Webb. It was enough to tempt Webb to send a spear into one of the snorkeler's legs.

But it wasn't a serious temptation. Webb wouldn't shoot someone from behind. He was sure he didn't even want to shoot the snorkeler. The spear gun, he told himself, was for self-defense.

Still, the rage burned inside him.

Webb closed in on the snorkeler and used his paddle to bang the back of the snorkeler's head.

That's all it took.

The snorkeler rolled over as Webb continued past him in the kayak, positioning himself between the snorkeler and the escape boat. Although he was easily out of reach of the snorkeler, he now had his back to the man. So Webb planted his paddle in the water and gave a reverse thrust to spin the kayak around.

He heard a *thunk* and felt a vibration.

Then felt disbelief.

There was a huge commando knife stuck squarely into the kayak, just below the waterline.

The kayak's momentum pushed the front of the kayak directly at the snorkeler, who was now standing in the waist-deep water.

Webb glanced at the knife and back at the snorkeler.

Webb was still safely out of range of the snorkeler's arms. He was at least forty feet away.

Webb lifted the spear gun.

"I'm going to tell myself you were throwing the knife at my kayak," Webb said, "and not at me.

Because I'm not sure you want me to be any angrier than I am right now."

Webb raised the spear gun and pointed it at the snorkeler.

"You don't have the guts," the snorkeler said. He pulled off his mask. Jack England. "You're just a kid."

Webb fired.

TWENTY-FOUR

The spear sizzled through the air in a slight arc, flashing sunlight for a brief moment.

It was Webb's javelin of fury.

It missed Jack England by at least five feet and hissed into the water behind him.

England laughed. He took a half step toward Webb.

Webb yanked the knife from the kayak and instantly realized that was a mistake. Water gushed into the hole.

England laughed again and took another step.

"I want you to think about your situation," England said. "If you want to use the knife on me, you're going to have to put the paddle down. Which I'll take. Or if you try to hit me with the paddle, I'll yank it from your hands. Either way, I'll have the better weapon."

Webb paddled backward, trying to keep distance between him and England.

"And if you keep going," England said, "either my boat is going to trap you, or you'll give me a path to the boat and I'm gone."

Webb pulled up his iPhone and pointed it at England.

"Wow," England said. "I'm scared."

He advanced on Webb.

Webb glanced back. The boat was too far away. England was thirty feet in front of him. To take more video of England, he'd have to sit where he was. To paddle the slowly sinking kayak, he'd have to give up the chance to video. And England was right. If Webb stayed between

England and the boat, Webb would be trapped. If Webb paddled to freedom, England was gone.

Webb gave a few hard paddles back toward the boat. As the kayak drifted, he picked up the iPhone again and hit *Video*.

"This footage will show that you were the snorkeler who fired at the dummy in the kayak," Webb said.

"Absolutely," England said. "It was great target practice. My name is Jack England, and I saw a dummy in a kayak and shot it with my spear gun."

"You didn't know it was a dummy," Webb said.

"Convince a judge of that," England said. He took a few more steps. They were awkward steps because of his flippers, but each step took him closer to Webb.

Now Webb was thirty feet from the boat behind him, and England was only twenty feet away. But at least Webb had both hands to paddle.

He threw the iPhone at England. It bounced off the man's shoulder and splashed.

"Idiot," England said.

"You wanted me and my grandfather on the charter boat that sank," Webb said. "Right?"

"Kid, really? You think I'm going to make some grand confession? Should have kept the iPhone to record it."

"You wanted us out of the way, right?" Webb said. "You're the one who used the nanny cam on Jonathan Greene, and you were afraid of what we'd learn."

"Sure," England said. "You happy? It won't do you any good. When I get in the boat, I'm going to run you down in your sinking kayak, because you won't get too far no matter how hard you paddle. So even if you have something in there like one of my cameras to record this conversation, I'll find it after I take care of you."

"You loosened the clamps on the seacock on the boat that sank," Webb said. That had been Robbie's guess. Robbie was the guide who'd taken the charter boat out instead of England. A seacock was a valve in the hull that was always supposed to be closed except when the boat was out of the water. "You disconnected the bilge pump and the bilge-pump alarm so the boat would fill with water and no one would notice until it was too late…right?"

Robbie said that's what he would have done if he wanted the boat to sink.

"I didn't want to drown you and your grand-father," England said. "You'd have been wearing life jackets. But something like that would have kept you out of my way for a day or two. And by then Greene would have been dead. I was worried about what he was writing down for you. I couldn't pick it up on the nanny cam."

Webb had kept paddling backward. Maybe twenty feet to England's anchored boat. Maybe ten feet between him and England. Webb would have to try to make his escape soon. But could he out-paddle a motorboat? Could he reach shallow water before the boat tore through his kayak?

"The nanny cam. Right," Webb said. "That was yours on the bedside table. Yvonne Delta finally got him to tell her about the diamonds, but you went first and took them before she could. Because she didn't know you were recording all the conversations."

That would explain why Yvonne Delta had shown no reaction to the nanny cam. She'd had no idea what it was. Or that Jack England had beat her to the diamonds' hiding place.

The kayak was still taking on water. Webb wasn't going to be able to move it to avoid an attack.

"What does this matter to you?" England asked. "Let me tell you something. When I didn't know it was a dummy in the kayak, I aimed left to take you in the shoulder. I just wanted you injured enough to either give me the diamonds or tell me where they were. But now, I think I'll run you over with the propellers of my boat. I can always say it was an accident if anyone ever proves it was me who hit you."

Ten feet to the boat, and ten feet between Webb and England.

Webb had little choice. England was correct. If Webb tried to use the knife, England would get the paddle. England was a far larger man. Webb wouldn't have a chance.

Webb made the choice.

He scooted the kayak away from the boat, giving England a clear path. He could feel the kayak lag with the water that had already filled it. There was enough Styrofoam in the kayak to keep it afloat no matter what, but as it filled with water, it would become clumsy and slow.

"How did you know that Yvonne was black-mailing him?" Webb asked.

England snorted. "One night when I went over to give him a report, I overheard her grilling him. That's when I set up the camera. Let me tell you, it was worth it. That first batch of diamonds has got to be worth a half million."

"Not to you," Webb said. He was safely out of reach now and well away from the boat. "It's all going to go to Operation Smile. Where Jonathan Greene wanted it to go."

England said, "Idiot."

"Maybe. Just so you know, I missed you on purpose with the spear gun. Shooting you wasn't part of the plan. But I thought if I missed, you'd think it was the best I had. That you would be overconfident and tell me stuff."

"Overconfident?"

"The plan was to put my kayak into water so shallow you'd have no choice but to kayak or snorkel to sneak up on it. My grandfather and I just wanted to know if it was you who had planted the nanny cam. The plan was to follow you back to the boat at a safe distance and have a conversation just like this."

"So I could mow you down with the boat after I got in it? Like I said. You're an idiot."

"Maybe not," Webb said. "There was another part to the plan. We wanted someone to listen to whatever you and I talked about."

England froze as there was movement on the boat. Of someone suddenly stepping onto the deck from below. Someone with a cell phone in one hand and a long fishing gaff in the other. It was Robbie, the resort's other fishing guide, the man with the mermaid tattoo.

"Jack," Robbie said in a conversational tone, "why don't you stay in the water for a while? I'm more than a little angry about you sending me out into the Gulf Stream in a boat you knew was going to sink, so I won't hesitate to hit you with this fish hook if you try to get in the boat. But you won't have to wait that long. I've got the Coast Guard on the way. And while we wait, maybe you can explain more about the diamonds the police found in your home about a half hour ago?"

TWENTY-FIVE

"When they brought your piece of cake, what did you wish for?" David asked Webb, who was taking his last bite of the chocolate dessert.

"That they'd only bring the cake and no one would embarrass me by singing," Webb said. The two of them were at Mickey's Sandbar restaurant, just before the Battle of the Bands.

David grinned. "I'm just glad you're safe. It's also nice to know that Jonathan's wish will be fulfilled when the police return the diamonds to Operation Smile."

Webb nodded. "And that second set, maybe it will never be found. But after this, you can bet people are going to be looking everywhere for it."

"Or maybe next year we could come back and look ourselves. I enjoy my time with you."

"And me with you, Grandpa," Webb said. "BBE."

"Huh?"

"This trip. Best birthday ever."

"Well, make it better," David said. "Go out there and break a leg. I'll be cheering for you. If you win, that will be rocking cool."

"Um…"

"Yes?" David said.

"Thanks," Webb said. He'd just used the phrase *BBE*. That was probably no different than someone his grandfather's age saying *rocking cool.* "I'm pretty motivated."

*   *   *

"You gonna burn, burn, burn, burn, burn to the wick. Oooh, barracuda…"

Barracuda, Webb thought, rubbing his arm where the stitches tugged against his skin. *A ferocious predator that relies on surprise to take down prey.*

Kristie's singing of the final words to the song reached Webb clearly where he was standing with a group of people at the bottom of the steps behind the outdoor stage near Mickey's Sandbar, which had sponsored the Battle of the Bands. The sun had set, but it was still hot. The slight breeze felt great to Webb.

Webb was wearing his Edmonton Eskimos T-shirt again. He had an electric guitar strapped to his shoulders. It wasn't plugged in, so as he ran through chords and arrangements, it made little noise. On the other side of the stage, the audience whistled and cheered after the final guitar riffs of "Barracuda." It lasted a full minute. That was a good sign for Kristie. Crowd reaction was one of the ways that the judges decided who would win the battle.

The lyrics of the song matched his new understanding of Kristie. *No right, no wrong...you lying so low in the weeds I bet you gonna ambush me...*

Moments later Kristie walked down the steps, followed by her lead guitarist, the guy with attitude named Sylas Grobell, who had told Webb to get lost the last time they met.

Kristie stepped onto the sand. There was enough light from the stage that she saw his face. She paused.

"Hey," she said.

"Hey," Webb answered in a flat voice, thinking of the song's beginning.

So this ain't the end, I saw you again, today I had to turn my heart away.

Kristie was a real barracuda. In disguise. At least with the first barracuda he'd faced in Florida, the danger was obvious. Razor teeth did a lot less damage than someone's deception.

If the real thing don't do the trick, you better make up something quick.

"Sylas," Kristie said, "stay with me, okay?"

Sylas stayed at her side and glared at Webb. "You again."

"Me again," Webb said.

"I should punch you," Sylas said. "My grandfather is in jail. All because of you."

Grandfather. If Webb had known the connection earlier, he might have understood sooner why Kristie kept showing up to ask questions about Jonathan Greene. Sylas was Jack England's grandson.

Webb shook his head with scorn. If Sylas couldn't accept that Jack England was in jail because of sinking a boat and stealing diamonds, no explanation from Webb would make a difference. And really, Jack England was in jail because of Kristie.

"Say it," Kristie told Webb.

"That I knew you would send Jack England out after me after I told you about the diamonds?" Webb answered. "Sure. I did."

Looking back, so much made sense. Jack England had listened to the conversation when Webb and his grandfather first visited Jonathan Greene. Greene had written things down, and England wanted to know what they were.

He'd heard that Webb had met Kristie. No coincidence that Kristie showed up in the night to ask Webb to go for a walk.

"You'd have done the same," Kristie said. "I got paid three hundred bucks to ask you a few questions."

As you held my hand and took advantage of knowing I had an instant crush on you, Webb thought. My first crush.

"I don't owe you an apology or anything," Kristie said.

Webb just shrugged. He wouldn't give her the satisfaction of learning how much it had hurt to finally figure it out. She'd kissed him on the cheek, a kiss he'd remember for a long, long time. But not with any kind of happiness.

From the stage came the voice of the local radio DJ who was helping with the Battle of Bands.

"Up next," the DJ said, "we have a kid from Canada who has promised us a few fun guitar licks."

Webb made to step by Sylas.

"You?" Sylas sneered. "We nailed it. You don't have a chance."

Webb gave Sylas a half smile. Webb wasn't a trash-talk kind of guy. He'd either do okay with the guitar or he wouldn't. If he did, the guitar would do enough talking. And if he didn't, anything he said to Sylas now would make Webb look foolish.

Webb took the steps two at a time. He should have felt nervous. Instead, he was fueled by cold anger.

He reached the spotlight and plugged in the guitar. It was a used guitar that his grandfather had rented for Webb. Webb had it tuned and ready to go. As he straightened, he saw that Kristie had climbed the steps to watch him from the back of the stage.

Cold anger. Yeah.

Webb faced the audience and spoke into the mic.

"My dad died a few years ago," Webb said. As he spoke, he played the guitar quietly, some sad and haunting chords. The crowd turned instantly quiet.

"And I miss him more than any amount of words can tell you."

This was Battle of the Bands. The crowd didn't want anything haunting and sad. The crowd wanted fast and loud. He'd get to it, but on his terms.

"My grandfather says that the people you love in your life never really leave you," Webb continued. He kept strumming chords, using the music background to underscore the emotions of his words. "Their actions become the fabric of your own life, so that they are always a part of you."

The spotlight was on Webb's face. Webb grinned. "My grandfather was right. Because my dad taught me this one."

Bang. Webb hit the opening riff to what he knew would be a crowd pleaser. The trick was to play stuff they knew, that they could get into.

He'd picked "La Grange," by ZZ Top.

That got a roar of applause.

"And my dad taught me this one," Webb said.

He ripped into the opening chords of "I Love Rock and Roll" by Joan Jett and The Blackhearts.

Webb had his medley planned, and he zipped through a series of dazzling guitar riffs in a high-energy session that had everyone in front of him standing and whistling.

He was rocking and he knew it.

The cold rage seeped away, and he found himself lost in the sound and the moment.

When he finished, he made sure it was an abrupt ending, leaving the crowd in a heart-beat of silence. And then there was an eruption of applause and whistling and cheering. It easily lasted for three or four minutes.

He might have won, and he'd find out soon enough.

But it wasn't about winning.

It wasn't about beating Kristie or Sylas. He wasn't going to care enough about them to allow them that kind of control over his life.

It wasn't even about being better than anyone else on that stage tonight.

It was about guitar. And honoring what his dad had taught him about guitar.

With the applause still at deafening volume, Webb lifted his right hand in a salute and spoke only to himself as the cheering and whistling continued.

"Dad," he said, knowing a few tears were leaking across his cheeks, "thanks for being here for me."

ACKNOWLEDGMENTS

To all my writer-in-residence story ninjas—
your help in reviewing the story was amazing.

SIGMUND BROUWER is the bestselling author of numerous books for children and adults, including *Rock & Roll Literacy* and titles in the Orca Echoes, Orca Currents and Orca Sports series. Sigmund and his family divide their time between his hometown of Red Deer, Alberta, and Nashville, Tennessee. *Barracuda* is the prequel to *Devil's Pass*—Sigmund's first novel in Seven (the series), which was a finalist for the John Spray Mystery Award, a Red Maple nominee and a *Kirkus Reviews* Critics' Pick.

THE SEVEN PREQUELS

HOW IT ALL BEGAN...

7 GRANDSONS
7 JOURNEYS
7 AUTHORS
7 ASTOUNDING PREQUELS

The seven grandsons from the bestselling **Seven (the series)** and **The Seven Sequels** return in **The Seven Prequels**, along with their daredevil grandfather, David McLean

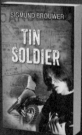

SEE WHERE WEBB GOES NEXT IN AN EXCERPT FROM **DEVIL'S PASS** FROM SEVEN (THE SERIES).

NOW

Beneath the vintage black Rolling Stones T-shirt he had found at a thrift store, Webb was wearing a money belt stuffed with $2,000 in prepaid bank cards. It was a lot of money for a seventeen-year-old who worked nights as a dishwasher. The belt cut into his skin as he sat against a building on a sidewalk in downtown Yellowknife, but Jim Webb didn't feel the pain.

Not with a Gibson J-45 acoustic guitar in his hands and a mournful riff pouring from his soul as he played "House of the Rising Sun," humming along to the words in his head. Webb was killing time before he had to catch a cab out to the airport.

Playing a guitar in a hotel room drew loud, angry knocks on the wall from the other guests, but playing on the street drew cash. That was one reason for the acoustic guitar—it was uncomplicated. Electric guitars needed amps and cords. The other reason was the sound. Just Webb and his guitar and his voice. What people heard was all up to him, and there was a purity in that kind of responsibility that gave him satisfaction.

Already half a dozen people had stopped to give him the small half-friendly smiles that he saw all the time—smiles that asked, "If you're that good, why are you sitting on a sidewalk with an open guitar case in front of you, waiting for money to be tossed in your direction like you're a monkey dancing at the end of a chain?"

Those looks never bothered him. Nothing bothered him when he had a guitar in his hands. For Webb, there was no rush like it. Playing guitar, hearing guitar, feeling the strings against the calluses on his fingers and thumb, watching people watch him as he played. All of it. No other way to describe it except as the coolest feeling in the world. Instead it was how he felt when the guitar was back in the case that worried him.